TWO GUN MARSHAL

Packing two guns, Jeff Bellamy comes to Red Rock to help his father's best friend, but finds Dorlen beyond help, and a town dying because its freight lines are being ruined. Tough man Bellamy dislikes small-timers being pushed around, so he stays. And, when the crooked marshal drops to a well-aimed bullet, takes over his job. But Red Rock comes perilously closer to its demise before its new marshal gets to grips with the instigator of all the trouble.

JOHN SAUNDERS

TWO GUN MARSHAL

Complete and Unabridged

LINFORD
Leicester

First published in Great Britain in 2010 by
Robert Hale Limited
London

First Linford Edition
published 2011
by arrangement with
Robert Hale Limited
London

British Library CIP Data

Saunders, John.
  Two gun marshal. - -
  (Linford western library)
  1. Western stories.
  2. Large type books.
  I. Title II. Series
  823.9'2–dc22

  ISBN 978–1–44480–552–9

Published by
F. A. Thorpe (Publishing)
Anstey, Leicestershire

Set by Words & Graphics Ltd.
Anstey, Leicestershire
Printed and bound in Great Britain by
T. J. International Ltd., Padstow, Cornwall

This book is printed on acid-free paper

1

The letter addressed to Tom Bellamy was a month old when Jeff, his son, received it.

Already toughened and made restless by the horrors of the Texan war in which his father had died of wounds Jeff acted on the instant. The letter from his father's closest friend, Carl Dorlen, seemed like an appeal for help, and Jeff did what he knew his father would have done. He made ready for the five hundred mile trip to Red Rock where Dorlen owned a saloon.

It seemed that Dorlen was having trouble; the kind that involved shots in the dark and unusually violent fights in his place. Jeff delayed only to buy a horse powerful enough to carry his weight long distances and to sink most of his remaining cash in a pair of Colts and a Winchester before hitting the trail.

At Durango, some sixty miles from Red Rock, Bellamy spent one night before going on. There, in apparently idle talk with a deputy named Sweney, he gathered quite a store of information concerning Red Rock.

The town's position on the map was uncertain, lying as it did where the States of Utah and Colorado met. The deputy's firm opinion that Red Rock was in Utah seemed based mainly on the fact that the town had trouble and Durango, which was comfortably within the borders of Colorado, had enough of its own brand of lawlessness. Sweney's closing remarks to Bellamy showed that the deputy was no greenhorn. His gaze went directly to Bellamy's twin Colts then lifted to stare into hard, blue eyes beneath the black Stetson.

'Mister,' Sweney said, 'you've been askin' a lot of questions an' you pack one more gun than usual. How come?'

'I've a friend in Red Rock. Feller named Carl Dorlen. Seems he might need some help.' Bellamy did not think it necessary to explain that he had never met Dorlen.

Sweney spat tobacco juice into the dust of the street. 'Dorlen don't need any help. They buried him more'n a month back. Had some kind of an accident, I heard. If it was the kind of accident that's gonna make for more shootin', keep out of Durango.'

Sweney gave Bellamy a flinty stare then turned away.

Red Rock was half a mile away when Bellamy hauled his mount to a halt and rolled himself a smoke. The dust-laden trail before him ran with moderate steepness down to an equally dusty collection of clapboard buildings, perhaps forty or fifty in number. Heat, dust and a general sense of torpor seemed to be the main features, not only of the town but of the arid and rockbound country at the sides of the trail. However, cow-towns were often built in the most unlikely places. Sometimes it depended on the twists and turns of the trail, at others, in the position of a waterhole. Quite frequently it was just that some pioneer had built in a particular spot for a purpose that had nothing to do with cattle.

Bellamy stubbed out his cigarette and kneed his mount forward.

Coming to the town he took in the lifeless aspect of the place. Almost deserted and with few horses at the hitch-rails it seemed to contain, besides the clapboard shacks, little else than one saloon and a frowsy-looking hotel. The street, not more than a few hundred yards long, forked at the further end and a timber building, larger than any of the others, stood where the roads branched. But, small as the town was, there ought to have been more life in it. What was it made the place so dead? What had caused all the trouble in such a two-bit dump? Dorlen's letter had suggested that a killer stalked the place. Now, Dorlen himself was dead. An accident — maybe.

Bellamy's mouth set in a grim line.

Things in Texas might have made him hard, even cynical and bitter, but it had certainly left him with a burning hatred of killers and law breakers. In a country where the law was staggering from the paralysing blows of war it was up to every two-handed man to hunt ruthlessly those who traded on the present weakness of justice.

He came level with the saloon, its newly painted sign reading Kerney's Saloon, and swung himself from the saddle. As he threw the reins over a rail three men made the small motions of men alerted and suspicious. The tallest of them, Red Malone, straightened up and passed through the batwings with the studied slowness of a man who has all the time in the world. His two companions, Buck Smith and Ab Lawson, gave unobtrusive hitches to their gunbelts and continued to stare at nothing in particular but at the same time missed no part of Bellamy's movements or of his equipment.

Neither man liked what he saw. This

tall rider now casually looping the reins over the hitch-rail was no ordinary cowpoke ranging the country for a job. Cowpokes did not usually tote the latest in Winchesters in a conveniently placed scabbard, neither did they wear a pair of Colts slung in tied-down holsters. This man now breasting the batwings spelled trouble and looked the kind who could make plenty.

The moment Bellamy disappeared into the saloon, Ab Lawson shambled hurriedly across the street to the office of Marshal Cain Hamble. A few moments later they both walked over to the saloon. Lawson remained outside as Hamble pushed open the batwings. Bellamy was at the counter, a mug of beer in his hand.

Hamble walked over to him. 'I'm the marshal. I like to know what goes on in this town.'

Bellamy took a leisurely drink. 'A good idea. I like to know what's going on myself.'

Hamble's face flushed darkly. 'Who

6

are you and what's your business in Red Rock?'

'Bellamy's the name. Jeff Bellamy — and my business is my own.'

'We don't cotton to strangers hangin' round this town without they has some business. Finish your drink and get movin'.'

'Yeah — or else?'

Bellamy's blue eyes regarded the marshal with interest but he did not move from his lounging position at the bar.

Hamble's hand flew to the butt of his gun. 'Or else I'll move you, that's what.'

Red Malone, who had been watching and listening from the far end of the bar, moved closer to Bellamy's back. He was less than a yard away when Bellamy straightened up casually, his drink in his right hand. Quite suddenly he lunged forward throwing the contents of the glass into Hamble's face. The same movement continued in an arc smashing the glass against Malone's face. Malone staggered back cursing and wiping blood from his face while Hamble spluttered and screwed up his eyes against the sting of the alcohol. Four or five men who had been seated at tables jumped to their feet while the tough-looking barkeep dived for the shotgun at the back of the counter.

Bellamy's hands went to his guns. 'Any of you guys that want to join in, come with your guns smokin'.'

In a moment the tension relaxed, the men who had been spectators went back to their tables. The barkeep moved deliberately away from his shotgun. Malone, dabbing furiously at a two-inch long gash in his cheek, went through the batwings. Hamble, his hand held well clear of his gun, glared angrily at Bellamy.

'We'll settle this another time, feller.'

'Any time you like.'

Bellamy turned his back on the marshal and called to the barkeep for another drink.

Hamble hesitated for a moment then passed out into the street.

Bellamy pulled at his glass then leaned towards the barkeep. 'What's it all about, feller?'

The barkeep, Joe Sangers, glanced at him nervously. 'Guess it's on account of the hold-ups. Hamble's plenty nervous about strangers.'

'Yeah? What hold-ups?'

'Holden's had three of his stages stuck up in the last month. Fellers that did it got clear away too. Not a sign of hide nor hoof. Holden owns the stage line. That's his place up at the fork.'

'How about the drivers, what happened to them?'

'Two of 'em dead, the other, Sam Moss, shot up so bad he ain't out of the doc's hand yet. Sam was the last one to git it.'

'Didn't any of the stages have a gun guard?'

'Nope. Holden couldn't git anyone to ride shotgun after the first killin'. Now he can't git anyone to drive for him either. Come to that he wouldn't have any passengers or freight, even if he did have drivers. Kin I get you another drink, Mister?'

Bellamy thought for a moment. He would have to get a job of some kind while he tried to find out just what had happened to Dorlen. Driving would be as good as any other. He said, 'No thanks, reckon I'll have a talk with Holden. I could use a job of some sort.'

Sangers studied Bellamy's back as he walked towards the door. Queer sort of stage driver, he thought. More like a road agent, with those twin guns.

Holden thought the same when Bellamy walked into his office and asked for a driving job. Holden's place, built on the fork of the street, was easily the biggest building in town. A month ago, Holden would have chased any stranger who dared to suggest picking up the lines of one of his precious stages or even of a freight wagon. Now, Holden was in no position to chase any man. In his present difficulty he would have been glad to let a drunken Indian drive one of his teams.

When he considered Bellamy's proposition to drive for him, Holden said: 'I've got to say yes and be darned glad about it, but I don't get it. Even if I were half blind I could see you're no ordinary team driver looking for a job. You're no cowpoke either. Still I don't see what I've got to lose. It's your risk. I'll take you — on suspicion. Sixty a month, take it or leave it.'

'I'll take it,' Bellamy answered 'Be all right if I stable in your place?'

'Sure. I'll show you the barn.'

Holden lifted his big bulk from the chair and with Bellamy a pace behind him walked out of the office.

Following his new boss, Bellamy took in the fact that the freight office, along with the barns and stables, formed a large triangular structure that split the end of the street into two. The office faced directly into the main street. Behind that was a loading bay that cut through from one fork street to the other, and behind the loading bay were the stables and barns. Three coaches

11

and six freight wagons stood in the barns, while from the stables sounded the restless movements of some dozens of horses.

Bellamy said, when Holden had finished showing him round: 'Quite a business you've got here.'

'Had,' corrected Holden. 'Ain't worth a plugged nickel now.' Suddenly he pulled up short and faced Bellamy, his lined and wrinkled face showing traces of heavy strain. 'Bellamy, I don't know much about you or why you're shoving your neck out by driving for me, but I'll tell you this. It's taken me the best part of forty years to build up this stage line — started it by packing freight with one wagon when the Indians were whooping it all over the country. If I don't get a clear run mighty soon, I'm finished.'

'How come the marshal don't fix a guard for you? Seems to me half-a-dozen riders with each stage ought to fix things.'

'Sure. If you could find half-a-dozen men in the town willing to risk having their hides punctured. Hamble reckons he can't find a single one to ride with him.'

'OK. Spread it around that tomorrow's freight leaves at the usual time. I'll fix me a room somewhere and see to my horse.'

Holden watched with a puzzled look as Bellamy stalked with long strides to where he had left his mount tethered, then with a shrug of his shoulders he turned into his office. Just where this newcomer fitted in was more than he could figure. However, he could do no harm, even if he did no good. Tomorrow's freight would not carry anything worth more than a dollar and hell knew how long it would be before he dared run a coach again. That was how scared the people of Red Rock had grown since the three hold-ups.

Bellamy stabled his horse, took a room in the Red Rock hotel, a two storied, clapboard building with a balcony that stood next to Kerney's saloon, then crossed the street to a frowsy lunch counter. The sign over the door told him that the place was owned by Seth Cavan and he guessed rightly that the bald-headed, stringy looking man wearing a dirty white apron was Seth himself.

The place was empty of other customers and Seth served the beef hash without comment but Bellamy noticed, as he ate, that Seth's eyes were never very far from himself. With the last mouthful of the hash swallowed Bellamy passed his mug for more coffee.

'You don't talk a heck of a lot,' he commented.

'Find it pays.'

'Would it strain you any to tell me where Sam Moss lives?'

'The second shack, east of the livery. Anyone in town could have told you.' Seth seemed about to clam up again but his normal desire for gossip got the better of him. 'Heard you were going to drive for Holden.'

'Sure, that's right. Didn't take long for you to learn about it. Who told you?'

'Folks figured it out for themselves. Holden let out that the freight will run tomorrow, an' there sure ain't anyone else in this town'll take a chance of drivin' for him.'

'Bad as that?' Bellamy got up from the counter. 'Don't let that tongue of yours get too free. It ain't healthy.'

He walked up to the shack Seth had indicated and knocked softly on the door. In the few seconds of waiting he noted the fresh curtains at the window and wondered what sort of a wife Sam Moss had. He gave a slight start of surprise when the door opened to show him a slim, dark haired girl of eighteen or nineteen whose figure was almost shrouded in an apron that was much too large for her. Bellamy touched his hat, he looked into eyes that were as blue as his own but deeply troubled.

He said in tones, gentle for him: 'I've come looking for Sam Moss.'

She glanced down at the twin guns. 'I'm not sure if — '

Bellamy cut in: 'Take no notice of the

hardware, ma'am. I just hired myself to drive stage for Holden an' thought I'd like a word or two with Sam.'

Instantly, she smiled. 'He'll be right glad to talk stages with anyone. Step right in, Mister — '

'Bellamy. Jeff Bellamy, ma'am. Sure glad to meet someone in the town who hasn't forgot how to smile.'

She stood aside as he entered. 'I guess folk in Red Rock are plenty worried at the moment. I'm Susan Moss — Father's in the back room and a bit grouchy because Doc won't let him go out of the house yet.'

Bellamy followed her into the back room and saw, hunched in a chair, a broad-shouldered man of no great height. Susan introduced the two men and then left the room to brew coffee.

As soon as the preliminaries were over Bellamy said: 'How an' where did it happen, Sam?'

Sam eased himself in the chair, giving little grunts of pain at the same time.

'You'll figure the place easy enough

tomorrow. Going east from here you'll swap teams at about twelve miles. Couple of miles after that you'll take a short rise then come on to a straight about five miles long an' the sides as bald and flat as a table. Just about half way along there it happened.'

'A mighty queer place to jump you,' Bellamy said.

'Yeah, I guessed you'd say that, everyone else does. I was making a pretty good clip when I saw a bunch of men ridin' towards me. Well there weren't nothin' to that an' the trail was plenty wide enough, so I just held on. On account of the dust they was raisin' I didn't notice they was all ridin' heads down. They was on top of me before I realized that every son-of-a-gun had a bandana tied across his face. 'Course, I reached for my shotgun but it was all over before I could think.'

'What about the passengers?'

'We only had two — coupla carpet-bag fellers from Durango. They didn't let out a squeak. Neither did I for that matter. I was rememberin' Spike Mulligan an' Jim Cameron an' how dead they were. Well, this bunch, there were five of them, cleaned everything out, then unhooked the hosses. I thought I was gettin' away with it until one of them turns a six-gun on me an' just about let me have the lot.'

Bellamy was still asking questions when Susan came in with coffee. He ceased his questioning as she poured and contented himself in watching her movements and listening to her comments on how bad things were getting to be in the town and how much worse it would be if the freight wagons did not soon start rolling, bringing in fresh supplies to the place. Not that there was as yet any real difficulty, she said, but the store was already nearly out of kerosene and it was surprising how quickly the stocks of tinned foods were disappearing.

Bellamy left after half an hour's chatting having, at the same time, gathered quite a store of information and made two good friends.

Crossing to the hotel, Bellamy saw Hamble coming towards him. Something in the marshal's movements indicated to Bellamy that he had been watching Sam Moss's shack and waiting for himself to come out. He made his own progress so that Hamble had to swerve to come up with him, then halted, waiting for Hamble to speak.

Hamble said: 'Forget about this morning, Bellamy. The way things are I'm mighty suspicious of strangers, more particularly when they're toting a pair of six-guns. I hear you've hired out to Holden — '

Bellamy allowed a long pause before saying: 'Sure, I guess everyone knows that now. It's OK with me if you want to forget this morning.'

He took a step forward that forced the marshal to one side.

Hamble said quickly: 'How if I fix for you to have a gun guard tomorrow?'

Bellamy halted and fixed cold eyes on the marshal. 'The other drivers didn't have a gun guard. How come you're so derned anxious to fix one up for me? I'll be hauling out at sun-up an' anyone that likes to ride with me can do so.'

Changing his mind about going to his room, Bellamy left the marshal and turned into Kerney's saloon. The place was beginning to fill now and Kerney himself lounged against the outside of the bar. He moved to where Bellamy had propped himself.

'Have it with me, Bellamy. Glad to know you.'

Bellamy took in the vast bulk of the man, amplified by the fancy waistcoat and the rolled up shirt sleeves.

'Thanks. Make it a beer.'

Kerney nodded to the barkeep, then said: 'So you're hauling for Holden? Hope you get through all right. My own stocks are getting mighty low.'

'But not low enough for you to do anything about it.'

'Meaning?'

'Meaning that, a town the size of this one ought to be able to raise enough guards to cover a stage line.'

Kerney pulled two cigars from his top pocket and handed one to Bellamy. Striking a sulphur match he regarded Bellamy acutely through his pig-like eyes.

'Someone's managed to throw a man-sized scare into this town. Mebbe you haven't heard the whole of the story.'

'I've heard that three of Holden's stages have been stuck up an' two of the drivers killed, an' I've seen Sam Moss who came near to ending the same way.'

'Holden didn't tell you about the accidents?'

Bellamy shook his head. 'What accidents?'

'Before the hold-ups, Holden's freight wagons had one trouble after another. A wheel would come off — lynchpin jump out — tug lines break. On one occasion a keg of blasting powder blew a wagon to pieces. So the fellers is just naturally scared to have anything to do with Holden.'

'Sounds like some *hombre* is trying to run Holden off the trail. Well, I guess I'll get some sleep. Mebbe I'll find out a whole heap more in the morning.'

Kerney nodded. 'Look after yourself, feller.'

It was almost dark when Bellamy stepped out of the saloon and walked the few paces to the hotel. The desk clerk nodded sleepily to him as he passed through the lobby and climbed the stairs. At the top he had to pause to accustom his eyes to the gloom of the long, narrow passage off which the bedrooms led on either side. A faint glimmer of light came from underneath one of the doors. Bellamy stiffened momentarily, realizing that the light came from his own room, then he cat-footed along the corridor and stood outside the door, holding his breath to listen for any sounds from within. After a moment he heard a faint shuffle of feet, then the sharp puff of breath given by the blowing out of the light. Bellamy stepped back and drew his Colt. A streak of twilight showed the edge of the door opening. Bellamy sprang towards it, his weight crashing the door wide and carrying whoever was behind it inside with a violent rush. He grappled with a dimly seen figure intent on using his gun as a club, then of a sudden changing his mind and flinging his adversary from him in the direction of the window, he rasped out:

'OK, no funny business. Light the lamp again an' let's have a proper look at you. There's matches on the table.'

The match flared smokily and even before it was touched to the wick of the lamp, Bellamy gave a grunt of surprise.

'Holy cats, I expected 'most anyone but you.'

Susan Moss turned a defiant face towards him. 'Let me pass.'

Bellamy holstered his gun. 'What makes you think you don't have to explain bein' here?'

'I came into the wrong room that's all. I — I wanted to see a friend of mine and — and — '

'You're lying like hell an' doing a bad job of it. Look at my war-sack an' tell me you haven't been mussin' through my things. Now come through, else I'll toss you over to the marshal as a common thief.'

For a moment Susan seemed to wilt then her chin lifted again. 'A fine tale that would be to tell the marshal. Go on, call the desk clerk and let him find us here together.'

Anger crossed Bellamy's face then turned to a grin. 'Why, you little she-devil. So you'd pull that old trick would you?'

Suddenly he grabbed her to him, holding her struggling figure easily with one arm, using his other hand to lift her chin upwards to plant a hard kiss on her lips.

Then he released her abruptly. 'Now you'll be able to say that you got what you came for.'

With a sob of anger she broke from him and raced down the corridor. Bellamy watched her flight, not in the direction he himself had come but towards a back staircase, the presence of which he would have suspected had he given the matter any thought. He closed the door and jambed a chair under the knob as a precaution, then dragged off his boots and, unbuckling his gunbelt, flung himself on the bed.

Taking it all round, his first day in Red Rock had been quite something. There seemed to be a lot to understand. No one had mentioned Dorlen's accident and Susan Moss entering his room was something he had not for a moment expected.

2

Bellamy sawed the four-horse team out of the dimly lit loading bay and turned it straight into the early rays of the sun. The contents of the wagon were not worth a handful of dollars but more in desperation than faith, some of the traders in the town had arranged for a good load of supplies to be freighted into town on the return trip. It seemed to Bellamy that the journey out and back might prove something. If he were jumped on the outward trip with a wagon that was almost empty it would seem to prove that whoever was behind the series of hold-ups was merely trying to drive Holden out of business. If on the return trip, then robbery might be the only motive.

Two men, Buck Smith and Ab Lawson trailed behind the wagon. Both carried rifles and were the gun guard the marshal had offered. Bellamy had seen the pair lounging outside the saloon when he had ridden into town and suspected that they might not be guards so much as reinforcements for the enemy. Beyond grunting a morning greeting to them he made no comment. Holden, however, seemed satisfied with the arrangement and had been of the opinion that the marshal was getting some of his sand back again.

Swinging the team through the town Bellamy thought mainly of Susan Moss and wondered why an innocent looking girl wanted to search through his things. He himself had nothing hidden in the hotel bedroom.

Clear of the town he shook the team up to a gallop which sent the almost empty wagon bounding and swinging over the ruts in the trail. He took three-quarters of an hour to reach the first stage and overlooked the changing of the team in silence. In the same silence he shook the new team into motion and shortly afterwards he sent it up the rise Sam Moss had told him of. Coming to the flat ground he eased the team down and used his eyes on the landscape. As Sam had said the place was as bald and featureless as a table top — one of those unaccountable level stretches that nature sometimes fits into otherwise rugged country. Well, if he were jumped here he should have plenty of notice of it, unless the attack came by someone overhauling him from the rear.

He gave an involuntary backward glance, surprising both of his guards in the same action. Suddenly the one he knew as Buck Smith gave a yell of alarm and dragged his gun from its holster. He yanked his mount completely round and, gun blazing, spurred towards two galloping horsemen, barely visible because of their distance. Ab Lawson glanced at Bellamy as if to make sure he had observed his partner's action then also spurred towards the distant figures.

Bellamy gave a thin, tight-lipped

smile. So this was the act. His two gun guards were clearing out, making it look as if they were fighting off the still distant men. If he himself won through the coming scrap it would be difficult to assert that his guards had quit on the job, even more difficult to accuse them of actually conniving at the hold up. Well, he might try a little play-acting on his own. He hauled hard on the reins and at the same time set up a whooping that could be heard a mile away. The team fought hard to break into a full gallop in obedience to his voice and just as hard, Bellamy held them back. In ten minutes of this performance the pursuers overhauled him rapidly and he had no need of backward glances to tell him that fact. Slugs whistling wildly past him were information enough. Now, Bellamy put on the second part of his own act. Suddenly he jerked upright in the driving seat and then slumped downwards out of sight of the galloping men. The team sawed from one side of the trail to the other bouncing first one wheel then another over some rock obstruction at the side of the trail.

The men following ceased shooting and concentrated their efforts in over-hauling the now really flying team.

Bellamy flattened on the floorboard and holding the lines in his left hand watched with satisfaction two riders who, one on either side, came level with the leading horses and reached out for the bridles. The wagon was almost at a standstill when he rocketed to his feet, a Colt in each hand.

The pair at the horses' heads, their faces masked by bandannas, found time to pull guns but the shots they fired were matched with the roar of Bellamy's twin Colts. Both left their saddles as if kicked out of them. One lay motionless with a small hole through his forehead, the other writhed and twisted on the ground.

Bellamy climbed down from the wagon and went over to him but even as Jeff reached him he ceased to writhe, and with a glare of hatred at the man who had shot him, passed the way of all men.

Bellamy turned to see if his so-called guards were in sight and saw them coming down the trail towards him at a not too hurried canter. When they reached him, surprise, not yet conquered, was evident in their faces. There was also more than a hint of fear in each man's expression.

Bellamy chose not to comment either on their actions or expressions and amused himself by watching their changing faces as he asked:

'Know either of these buzzards?'

Each in his own fashion denied having any knowledge of the dead men or of the brand the riding horses carried.

'Don't suppose it matters any. The horses were probably stolen anyway. Best thing you fellers can do is load these stiffs into town an' let the marshal have a looksee at them an' their horses. It ain't likely I'll be worried again this trip. I reckon whoever's behind the business might be a bit short on men at the minute.'

'You don't reckon these fellers organised the thing on their own then?' Ab ventured.

Bellamy's, 'No, I don't,' made both men shift uncomfortably in their saddles and under his gaze they climbed down and started to load the dead men on to their own mounts.

Bellamy watched the last knot tied then climbed to the wagon seat.

'Don't lose those stiffs on the way,' was his last comment delivered in a dead flat voice as they set off back for Red Rock.

There was another eight miles to cover to the next changing place. Bellamy knew it slightly, having stopped there on his way into Red Rock. Besides having a barn for the stage horses the place had a lunch counter and could serve a hurried snack to passengers wanting one. From what Holden had said the couple running the place were Zeke Smethers and his wife, Dolly.

Bellamy had seen Zeke, a surly, middle-aged groucher, and imagined Dolly to be about the same age with possibly a similar temperament. He was therefore surprised when he hauled the team to a halt, to see a brassy-haired young woman, somewhat voluptuously built, come to the door of the shack. She gazed at him with an unwinking stare for a moment then switched on a brilliant smile.

'Hello there, stranger. Got time to eat and stretch for a spell?'

'Yeah, I guess so.'

Zeke came out from the barn and started unhooking the lathered team. He took a long stare at Bellamy but did not speak.

Dolly gave her husband a contemptuous glance then switched on her smile again for Bellamy's benefit.

'Bacon an' eggs do?'

She let her eyes rove appraisingly over Bellamy's tall frame.

'Sure, that'll do fine.'

Bellamy followed her into the shack,

sure that she was giving an extra swing to her hips especially for his benefit. Not averse to a little feminine by-play he grinned at her back, then tried to straighten his face as she turned her head suddenly.

'Not bad?' she enquired, a mocking light in her eyes.

'Better when I get some grub inside me,' grinned Bellamy.

'Like all the others,' she jeered. 'Grub first, last an' all time.'

She bustled to the stove and in a few minutes served him with a well cooked meal. Bellamy ate hungrily enough, listened to her banter, which was all laced with a hint of sex, and when his mouth was not full made suitable replies. Zeke looked in twice during the meal, glowering at his wife on each occasion. He came a third time and informed Bellamy that the team was waiting. Bellamy got to his feet, paid his score and with a last grin at Dolly, walked outside.

The trail before him curved sharply

away from the stage buildings and as soon as Bellamy was in the seat he lashed the team to the usual frenzied gallop that would be expected of him. The moment he was round the bend, however, and out of sight of the shack he hauled on the lines and set the drag. Climbing down he inspected first the four wheels and the drag then the lynch pins. Next he went over the tug lines and somehow was not surprised to find one of them neatly sliced to near breaking point.

He made emergency repairs with some rope that was in the wagon then set the team in motion again. Over the next stage, which had plenty of up grades, any one of which would probably have broken the sliced tug and sent the team floundering over the sheer edge of the trail, Bellamy did a lot of thinking.

The tug line had certainly been all right when he had left Red Rock. He had checked every point himself just before climbing to the driving seat.

That seemed to mean that Zeke Smethers or Dolly was responsible. Zeke, of course, had had ample time to do the job — Dolly — well, it was just possible. There had been a brief space when she had left the shack but Zeke had been outside at the same time, so it could hardly be her responsibility alone. Of course there was the possibility of some third party.

Coming in for the next change of horses Bellamy decided to say nothing about the tug having been cut. With the strain that had been on it, it looked, by now, as if it might have been broken by wear and there was no point in disclosing that he knew otherwise.

An elderly man Bellamy knew as Jenks had charge of this changing post. He looked at the damaged tug with eyes that were beginning to fail.

'You bin lucky you didn't break your neck,' he commented. 'If that line had a bust goin' uphill, I reckon Holden woulda lost another wagon as well as a driver.'

Bellamy shrugged the matter aside and helped to hook in the new team. He was away again from the halt in less than ten minutes after he had hauled in and set the fresh horses to a mile-eating pace that brought them to Durango without further incident.

Lincoln Jones, otherwise just Lin, was Holden's agent in Durango. He greeted Bellamy with some surprise and his eyes immediately went to the twin guns Bellamy wore.

'Holden decided to shoot his way through?'

'Something like that. Holden wanted a driver an' I wanted a job, so we sort of fitted in.'

Bellamy took in Lin's long, stringy figure and leathery face and decided that he liked the man. Decided that, in spite of the city clothes the man had seen many a hundred miles of team hauling before he had turned himself into a freight agent.

As Lin led the way into his office he said: 'Have any trouble coming up?'

'Some. A couple of guys tried to jump me — a little ways after the first change.'

'On that flat, bald stretch?'

'Yeah. You know the place?'

'Know every trail for three hundred mile around.'

Bellamy grinned. 'I figured you would. Mebbe you can tell me why they picked a place like that to try and jump me.'

Lin shook his head. 'Haven't a notion. What happened to the guys?'

'They got in the way of bullets I was firin'.'

'Yeah. I figured *that* about you.'

Both men laughed. Then Lin turned serious. 'I hope you can make it with this load. It'll just about finish Holden if you don't. The stuff's going at his risk and he's already paid out plenty over the other stick-ups and accidents.'

Bellamy shot an oblique question. 'Who stands to gain on the deal if Holden goes out of business?'

'Been trying to figure that one out for

myself. Of course, Wells Fargo will horn in if Holden does get flattened but it's no use thinking they'd try to force him out in that way. Holden did have an offer from them for the line, but shucks, that's nearly a year ago. Holden turned the offer down flat and hasn't heard a single thing about it since. When're you aimin' to pull out — first thing in the morning?'

'No. I reckon I'll get movin' as soon as you can fix a load.'

Lin gave him a sharp glance. 'OK, get yourself something to eat. I'll have the wagon loaded in less than an hour but it'll be plumb dark by the time you get to Zeke's place.'

Bellamy nodded. 'I reckoned on that.'

It was, as Lin had forecast, plumb dark. Bellamy had kept this team, the second one since he had left Durango, at little more than a walking pace and now, within a few hundred yards of Zeke's place, he set his foot on the drag and climbed down to the trail. The shacks and barns were a barely distinguishable hump of shadow as he made his way on foot towards them. The door of the horse barn opened with a slight grating noise as he pulled. For a minute he waited, watching the shack in case the slight sound had been heard, then he stepped into the even darker interior. A horse moved restlessly. Bellamy spoke in low, soothing tones and then struck a match. In the brief moments of light he counted eight horses in their stalls. Two riding saddles were over a rail close to him. Carefully extinguishing the last red glow of the match he took the two steps that brought him alongside the saddles. His fingers explored beneath the saddle-flaps, then he moved out of the place. Zeke had company that had arrived not long since. Both saddles had still been warm underneath.

Bellamy closed the door as quietly as he could, waited until he was certain that the occupants of the shack had not been disturbed then moved quickly back to the wagon. He set the team into motion, jerked out one of his guns and fired three shots in the air. As soon as the team had reached a gallop he emptied the gun, splitting the night silence with echoing roars. Almost outside the stage buildings he used his second gun and accompanied the shots with a tirade of violent language. When, a few moments later, the door of the shack jerked open Bellamy was on the ground ramming fresh cartridges into his weapon. He triggered off one more shot and then jumped for the doorway, his rush carrying inside again three dimly seen figures. On the instant he jammed the door to and yelled for a light to be lit. As the others stumbled about in the darkness Bellamy stood with his back to the door. A match spluttered and flared and finally a kerosene lamp glowed.

Zeke grumbled: 'What the hell's goin' on?' Then his eyes took in the fact that Bellamy was the new arrival and he stopped short.

Bellamy was not looking at him but

at the faces of Smith and Lawson. He said, without taking his eyes off the pair:

'Some coyotes tried to dry-gulch me a little way back — ' and did not miss the start of surprise given by both men.

Turning his gaze on Zeke he saw that he was trying to frame some suitable remark but could find none.

Finally, Zeke muttered: 'You aimin' to finish in town tonight? If so I'd better see to them hosses.'

Bellamy switched his gaze quickly to the two guards and saw the beginnings of hope in their eyes. He said as if he were tired:

'No, I guess not. I'll pull out come sunup. Mebbe these two gents will ride guard back to town.'

As if the thought had just occurred to him, Lawson said: 'Sure, that's what we came for, but we weren't expecting you to leave Durango before dawn. Hamble said, after we'd toted those stiffs into town, to get after you an' ride guard on the way back.'

'Sure, that'll be dandy.' Bellamy gave a yawn. 'I'm plumb tired. I'd sure appreciate if you guys'd run the wagon into a barn and help Zeke see to the horses.'

After a slight hesitation both men followed Zeke outside. Bellamy crossed to the stove and fingered the coffee pot to check if it was still warm. It was, so he looked round for a mug. Then the door at the far end of the room opened and Dolly walked in. Although she wore only a wrapper over her night-dress it was obvious from her carefully arranged hair that she had spent some time in preparation of herself. She gave Bellamy a brilliant smile.

'Well, glad to see you back so soon. I'll fix that coffee for you. How about somethin' to eat?'

'No thanks. Just the coffee.'

She took a mug from a cupboard then moved closer to him than she needed in reaching for the coffee pot. Bellamy's nostrils were filled with her cheap scent. As he took the mug from her, her lips moved quickly.

'Watch out for those two buzzards, han'some — an' Zeke as well.'

Just at that moment Zeke pushed quietly into the room and glared at his wife.

'Ain't no call for you to be out of bed,' he rasped at her.

3

Hamble's office, provided for him by the town when they had hired him as marshal, consisted of one room fronting on to the main street and a little pen at the back which he used on occasions to house men who got drunk enough to resist his ideas of keeping order. With Buck Smith, Ab Lawson and Hamble himself, the little office was just about filled.

Hamble was angry and showed it both by his scowling face and tone of voice. He glared at the other two.

'If you two guys can't take care of Bellamy I'll have to do it myself.'

Lawson said: 'Well, we tried, but jeese, how were we to know that the guy would turn right round at Durango and come back in the dark?'

'You should have figured that,' Hamble growled. 'Anyone could have seen he's a smart guy. The kind that thinks of everything. What I can't make out is how he came to horn in on the game. What's in it for him? Holden'll sure give him somethin' of course, but not enough to make a guy want to stick his neck out as far as he's doin'. Where is he now? Sleeping it off in his room?'

'I reckon so,' Smith answered. 'He's planning to run another freight wagon out about noon, us two ridin' guard again.'

'OK then. This is what we do. Let him get clear of town an' change teams at Zeke's place. I'll ride out ahead of him and be waiting for him just where the trail curves uphill. He won't have much speed on then and I can get him easily with a rifle. That ought to discourage anyone else who wants to drive for Holden.'

'Make sure you don't miss,' warned Lawson. 'That guy's poison with those guns of his. Me an' Buck seen him in action.'

'Me? Miss with a Winchester at forty

or fifty yards? Don't talk so plumb foolish.'

The pair left the office anxious to catch up a little of their own lost sleep and crossed the street to the shack they shared together.

Bellamy's room window did not look out on to the street, which was why he was sitting in the gloomy lobby of the hotel while the nervous desk clerk, scared to death of Bellamy's twin guns, watched Hamble's office and reported its coming and goings.

When the clerk notified him of the departure of Smith and Lawson, Bellamy sank back in the swivel chair and closed his eyes.

He said in his most ferocious tones: 'Now keep watching for Hamble, an' the moment he comes out of the office see which way he goes an' then wake me up. If you miss him or talk to anyone I'll fill you that full of holes they'll be able to use you for a sieve.'

The clerk shivered and said: 'Yessir, Mr Bellamy. Whatever you say. You go right on sleeping, Mr Bellamy. I'll keep right on watching.'

Bellamy snoozed comfortably until an hour before noon then wakened with a jerk, conscious that the clerk was moving towards him.

'Just come out of the office and rode west.'

'West!' Bellamy said sharply, then grinned.

If Hamble was up to anything it was only a natural precaution to ride west until he was out of the town and then circle round and pick up the east trail at some point. He went out of the place, reminding himself that, while he did not like Hamble and certainly had reason to distrust his choice of guards he had not even the smallest evidence that the marshal was playing it crooked.

Almost on the point of entering Holden's office he came face to face with Susan Moss. She gave him one sharp glance and then with lowered eyes made to move quickly to one side. Bellamy shot a long arm out and caught her wrist in a firm grasp.

Susan's face lifted, flushed and angry. 'Let me go. How dare you?'

Bellamy grinned. 'Seems we both dare plenty. How if you tell me what you were doing in my room? Whatever it was you didn't find it, did you?'

Susan made a vain attempt to wrench free. 'You're hurting me, and there's old Mrs Hendon watching us. She'll spread it all round town about us fooling together.'

'Don't run away from me then,' Bellamy warned releasing her. 'Now tell me about Sam. How's he getting along?'

Some of the anger died from Susan's face. 'Oh, Father's making great headway. The doc reckons he'll be as good as new in two or three weeks.'

Bellamy smiled. 'That's fine. Now tell me what you came to my room for.'

Once again came the defiant, angry look. 'I won't.'

Bellamy's hand closed on her wrist again. 'I've a mind to kiss you while

Mrs Hendon's watching. Teach you not to fool around with danger, but I guess I can find most things out for myself.' He let go of her wrist. 'Tell Sam I'll be in to see him after this run.'

He touched his hat and watched her walk away before going into the office.

Holden greeted him enthusiastically. 'Weren't sure you'd want to make another haul after last night's do.'

'Well, I told you I would.' He said nothing of half expecting another 'do.'

Holden rattled on. 'One or two folks talking about ridin' the stage into Durango since you cleaned up those two hombres. That is, if you'll drive it.'

'Better see how this trip goes. I see my two guards ridin' this way. Is the wagon loaded?'

'Yep. Loaded an' they're hookin' the team on right now. Told them to when I saw you talkin' to Susan Moss.'

Bellamy walked with him into the loading bay and assured himself that there were no loose pins or partly severed tug lines before he climbed to the driving seat. Wheeling the team out to the street his mind was filled with thoughts of Susan. Somehow, in spite of her strange actions, he felt no suspicion of her. Something, he told himself, that must be cured. Susan seemed a real nice girl, but —

Smith and Lawson swung their horses so as to come behind the wagon. Bellamy, on a sudden idea, applied the drag sharply, bringing the wagon to a halt.

He turned round on the seat. 'How if one of you fellers rides in front? That way we'll be in better shape to deal with anyone that tries to jump us.'

He read in their eyes reluctance to ride ahead of the team. It could be cowardice or it could be that the move would break up some plan of their own.

Suddenly, Smith urged his mount forward. 'I'll ride in front as far as Zeke's place then we can change round.'

Bellamy saw the sudden flash of anger that came into Lawson's eyes and read in it that whatever plan was afoot would not be put into action before they reached Zeke's shack. He let go the drag and, with a wild yell to the team, started them at a furious gallop, a pace he kept up until the first stage was reached. With a fresh team hooked in he arrived at Zeke's place almost a quarter of an hour before he could be expected. Determined to act as usual he passed inside the shack with the two guards clattering at his heels. Dolly was slow to show up and when she did so, the reason was obvious. One side of her face was swollen and red.

Smith grinned at her. 'Hi, Dolly. Been kicked by a hoss or did Zeke tell you to stop smiling at the customers?'

Dolly turned on him, sullen anger in her eyes. 'Mind your own goddam business, can't you?'

Smith gave a gusty laugh and reached a hand towards her. 'Hey, you don't havta act up, Dolly. Me an' you's — '

Dolly's hand cracked against the side of Smith's face. In a second, rage flamed up in the man.

'Why you bitch, I'll — '

His hand raised to strike a blow. Instantly, Bellamy lunged at Smith sending him reeling across the floor.

'You heard what the lady said. Lay off her.'

Smith's hand grabbed at his six-gun. Bellamy stood, feet a little apart, hands a few inches from the butts of his guns.

'Go on, make your draw,' he invited softly.

Smith hesitated for a moment then with a muttered curse his hand came away from the gun. He glared malevolently at Bellamy and then turned away. Dolly turned as if nothing unusual had happened and started to serve the meal. In a quarter of an hour's time Zeke put his head in the doorway and grunted that the team was waiting. Bellamy walked outside followed by his two guards. He took time to examine the wagon before climbing to the driving seat. Smith and Lawson had both stationed themselves at the rear of the wagon. Bellamy gave the thinnest of smiles.

'I thought we arranged for one of you hombres to ride in front of the team?'

Neither man answered.

Bellamy shrugged his shoulders. 'Tell you what — suppose you both get up front?'

Both men stiffened. Bellamy said, in a voice totally devoid of expression. 'I suggest you two gents get in front.'

A split second of hesitation and then the pair moved their horses forward.

Bellamy whipped the team into action. As they took the long curve and started to climb Bellamy noticed two things. The pair in front of him were crowding on the pace, also they rode so widely apart he could have easily driven the team right between them. The smile that had put a slight curve to Bellamy's mouth died out to be replaced by a thin-lipped tenseness.

It took almost no intelligence to realize that the pair in front were expecting some kind of an attack on himself and the wagon. The question was — where and how would it happen? He lashed the team to a greater pace in an effort to draw nearer his guards, but from time to time one or the other of them glanced backwards and the distance increased rather than diminished.

Bellamy read in the move the desire of the pair to keep well away from him. From that it certainly did not look as if an ordinary stick-up — an affair of three or four mounted men — was intended.

Bellamy kept his eyes on the men in front. Now, the frequency of their backward glances increased and both were using their spurs. He hauled the team to an easy pace and reached down for the Winchester beneath his feet. The ground ahead was devoid of cover except for one small hump of rock with which his two guards were almost level. Bellamy hauled harder on the reins bringing the team to a slow walk up the steep hill. The guards were past the hump of rocks and no longer driving their mounts.

'Feel themselves safe,' Bellamy muttered to himself as he jammed his foot on the drag.

The wagon came to a halt and a moment later one of the men in front gave yet another backward glance then he and his companion halted.

Bellamy's thin smile came back. He got down to the ground and sauntered along the side of the wagon, apparently intent on examining the wheels. From time to time he glanced in the direction of the two guards. Neither of them had moved. He straightened up and waved to them and then pointed at one of the front wheels indicating that he was having some kind of trouble. Still neither guard came towards him. He reached for the Winchester, clear in his own mind now that someone waited behind the low hump of rock. It had to be that way, there was no other cover in sight and the two men supposedly there to guard him from attack had pulled up reasoning that they were out of the way of anyone shooting from behind the rock. Bellamy took note of the distance to the rock. Near enough to six hundred yards. An easy shot for a marksman but difficult for an average shot.

Was the man behind the rock better than average? There was only one way to find out and Bellamy took it. Leaving the trail he walked straight for the hump, the Winchester apparently carelessly held. He covered two hundred yards with his eyes fixed on the rocks before he saw a movement. On the instant he flattened to the ground and in the same moment a slug whanged off the hard rock to his right. Bellamy's thin smile widened to a grin. The man behind the rock had made his play and failed. Bellamy counted him already dead. Cautiously, he crawled back until he had doubled the range between himself and the gunman. Several more slugs came near him as he moved but when he finally stood up the silence was complete. Evidently the man who had tried to drygulch him considered the range too great.

Bellamy moved in a wide half circle that came away from the trail and kept the hump of rock about the same distance from him. He spared scarcely a glance at his two guards who did not seem to have moved but concentrated his attention on the spot the shots had come from. This was a stalking game and he had plenty of time in which to play it.

He made a quarter circle before the man behind the rock made a move. A move that was his last. In scuttling to another position the man showed Bellamy perhaps six square inches of himself for the split part of a second. Long enough at any rate for Bellamy to throw the rifle to his shoulder, take a lightning sight and squeeze the trigger.

Before the shot echoed, the gunman behind the rock jerked convulsively upright only to slam down again as Bellamy's second shot went between his eyes, which was just exactly where Bellamy had aimed it. Bellamy gave a glance at the two guards as he closed in on the dead man. They started to move and reached the place before he did. They were still in their saddles when he came up to them.

Lawson and Smith had never seen the dead man before. Hamble had obviously got someone else to do the job.

Bellamy said casually: 'Know this buzzard?'

Both men denied rapidly and in voices that confirmed the expression of surprise on their faces.

'Well, I guess it don't matter a cuss. He won't give any more trouble. Suppose one of you high-tails it back to Zeke's place and have him make some arrangements to get the guy planted?'

Smith said immediately: 'Sure, Bellamy. I'll go. I'll soon catch up with you again, Me an' Ab was kinda puzzled when you hauled to a halt. Course, we didn't see this guy an' — '

'Sure, I get it. There ain't no need to explain. Nothing to explain, I guess. Guy gets behind some rocks an' tries to jump me. The guy loses out. I guess that's about all.'

Turning away he saw the puzzled glances pass between Lawson and Smith. Something more than his apparent failure to see their own connection with the attempt to kill himself was worrying them. He guessed it was the identity of the dead man. They had expected to see someone else. Whether they knew the dead man was something he could not decide but he was certain it was not the man they had counted on seeing.

Later, when Bellamy pulled into Durango he talked the matter over with Lincoln Jones.

Lin said thoughtfully: 'It don't stack up, Jeff. It just don't stack up. Have you figured how much this hold-up business is costing whoever's running it and how much he stands to gain by it?'

'I'm not so good at figurin' that way,'

Bellamy admitted.

'Well, look at it this way. There's never been less than three or four men on the job at any time. You yourself cleaned up a couple one time and then there were those two coyotes you've got with you as guards. That's a tidy pile of dough going out. Holden's trade just ain't worth that much and his losses in dead horses and broken wagon stock don't make him any richer prize.'

'Something more behind it then? Something I've gotta find out before I can clean this deal up.'

'That's about the size of it — ' Lin hesitated.

Watching him, Bellamy smiled slightly. 'Go on — say it.'

'Well, it's kind of personal, but I guess I've just got to ask. What's in it for you, Jeff? No one in town's going to pay you — except, that is, what Holden pays you for driving freight. I reckon you could make that much anywhere without chancing your neck?'

Bellamy said nothing for a minute,

then: 'If that wagon's loaded I'd like to get movin' again.'

Lin nodded and led the way out to the loading bay. In a few minutes the loading was completed and Bellamy climbed into the seat. His two spurious guards waited outside already in their saddles. Bellamy held the team in as they pulled out and made the turn into the main street. He glanced round to wave to Lin and at that moment a rifle cracked sharply, the slug chipping wood at Bellamy's side. He left the seat in a rolling movement, the reins still tight in his hands. He hit the dust just behind the hoofs of a wheel horse which immediately lashed out a vicious kick. Another shot came whistling to plunk in the dust near Bellamy's head at the wheeler's hoofs. Again the animal kicked savagely and then snapped its teeth at its mate. A second later the whole four horses were kicking and squealing in their rage. The wagon started to move. Bellamy, hanging on to the reins, saw his danger. He had fallen so that he was between one of the front wheels and the hoofs of the nearest horse. If someone did not get at the horses' heads there was more than a chance that the heavily laden wagon would pass over him.

He tried to squirm to one side while still keeping his weight against the reins. In the movement he had a glimpse of two other horses wheeling to the side of him. There was a burst of six-gun fire, maddening to a greater degree his already plunging team. He heard men shouting and a woman's scream, then running feet. Another burst of shots came then the reins he had been hauling on so grimly went slack in his hands.

Aware now that others had hold of the frightened horses Bellamy flung himself from beneath the wheels and rocketed to his feet. Lawson and Smith were circling round on their own mounts and both men held smoking guns in their hands. As Bellamy dusted himself down a man with a deputy's badge came hurrying towards him.

'What's all the ruckus, feller?'

Bellamy explained about the two rifle shots and showed the deputy the clean, new groove in the side of the wagon seat.

Lawson, still mounted, edged his way forward. 'Some guy hidin' in that alley over there.' He pointed to an alley directly opposite. 'Me an' Smith caught a sight of him when he fired that second shot, so we both cut loose with our irons.'

The deputy said: 'Well, there ain't much to go on, but I'll look into it.' He looked directly at Bellamy. 'If you ain't hurt none, feller, this town would sure appreciate if you got the hell out of it. We're plumb sorry about Holden's troubles but we don't want any shootin' 'round here. Got enough of our own worries.'

Bellamy nodded. 'Sure, I get it.' He dusted himself a little more then climbed to the seat. To the men who had been holding the heads of the team he shouted: 'OK, fellers, let 'em go, an' thanks for the help.'

Coming out of the town Bellamy gave some thought to the recent incident. That Lawson had been lying was certain. The bullet that had cut the groove in the side of the seat had come in a downward direction and at quite a steep angle. Most likely it had been fired from one of the flat roofs opposite to where the wagon had been standing. It would seem then that the shots fired by Lawson and Smith had been with the deliberate intention of further maddening the already scared team. Any small doubts he might have entertained about which side his two guards were on could be dismissed. Did it follow that Hamble, the town marshal, was also on the side of the hold-up gang? It seemed possible. Hamble had provided the two men. Lin had made a big point also. What *was* the main purpose behind all the skulduggery? Something more than just an attempt to drive Holden out of business, Bellamy felt certain of that.

Did any of it tie up with the death of Dorlen? Dorlen's letter had told of shots in the dark and savage fights in the saloon that might have put him out of business. But who stood to gain by Dorlen's death? Apparently, only Kerney — if taking over a down-at-heel saloon in a town that was falling apart could be called gain.

4

Dead tired though he was when he threw himself on his bed after the long haul from Durango to Red Rock, Bellamy woke with a sensation of something wrong.

Instantly his hand reached for the gun at his side. Then his fingers relaxed. He had not wakened to any sound, it was some other sensation not yet grasped. He swung his feet quietly to the floor and then lifted himself from the bed. A thin moonlight illumined the room and showed nothing unusual. For a moment he thought he had been deceived into wakefulness, then his nostrils caught a faint, acrid smell and a moment later identified it as burning kerosene. It took him less than a minute to drag on some clothes and get himself into the street. Here, the night breeze brought the smell of burning strongly to him and gave him direction.

As he ran down the street little puffs of smoke rolled to meet him. Then he caught sight of flames licking at the structure of Holden's sprawl of wooden buildings. In his final rush towards the place he yanked out a Colt and split the silence of the night with a burst of gunshots and followed the shots with loud yells of 'fire!'

Haring round to the side of the building the squealing and stamping of frightened horses came loudly. Bellamy gave a wrench at the doors of the loading bay, then guessing they were probably barred from the inside, tore round to the small side entrance. That also was locked but he crashed his shoulder again and again at the door until it burst inwards under his weight. Choking clouds of smoke rolled out of the shattered doorway as he floundered into the interior. Coughing and spluttering he paused for a moment to get his bearings. He was on one of the three-feet-high loading platforms. Somewhere to his left was a stairway leading to Holden's living quarters, to his right the platform ended near the big doors, and on the opposite side of the bay were the stables from which came a continuous frightened squealing. From outside he could hear the shouts of other men roused by his gunshots. He decided rapidly that if the main doors were unbarred there would be plenty of help to get the horses out first. Holden himself, if not already roused, soon would be.

He edged through the thick smoke along the narrow platform, misjudged its length and went floundering off. Cursing and coughing alternately he picked himself up and groped for the big doors. Finding them he tossed the bar out of its cleats and dragged the doors wide open. He had a brief sight of excited men outside running towards him and then, without warning, red and yellow flames leapt from every direction. Instinct warned him to run into the street, away from the furnace that the gusts of night air had brought into being. He obeyed instinct, then as suddenly remembered the horses and doubled back into the crackling flames. His first rush carried him far inside and now there was no lack of light to see where he was going.

With clothing scorching in a dozen places he reached the door of the stables. The surrounding woodwork was well alight but the door itself was only smouldering. The sounds coming from inside made it seem as if every fiend in hell had broken loose. He lifted the wooden latch on the door and immediately a wild-eyed, snorting animal dashed out knocking him mercilessly to one side with its powerful shoulders.

Bellamy rebounded off the blazing woodwork with most of the breath knocked out of him then plunged into the screaming, stamping hell of terrified horses. He grabbed at the slip hitch of the first head-rope, beat the animal backwards from the stall and, dodging its whirling hoofs, drove it through the doorway. Moving from stall to stall he chivvied and beat at over a dozen horses, his own included, until they had all plunged into the loading bay. Making for the doorway himself he discovered that, far from being out of danger the horses were in a worse plight than before. In the stables there had been only a choking smoke. Out here in the loading bay the flames leapt high, making the passage to the doorway a place of greater terror to the horses.

Bellamy, half blinded with smoke, scorched and seared in a dozen places, danced about among the animals beating at them with his fists, clubbing them with a gunbutt, trying every way to stampede them through the flames into the open. Two or three, more scared of him than of the flames, made a squealing, wild-eyed dash to safety. Bellamy turned his attention to a big gelding, a savage beast who could never be persuaded to run unless it was in the lead. He had some idea that if this great beast could be persuaded to bolt for the entrance door, the others might follow it. He made a grab at the head rope.

The gelding reared, then brought down its massive forefeet with a squeal of rage. Apparently it must have decided that Bellamy himself was responsible for its present suffering, for on him making a second grab for the rope it ran at him with bared teeth and rolling eyes.

Bellamy dodged, tripped on something and went down with a crash, the gelding raised on its hind feet to bring its forefeet down in a killing smash. Bellamy made a desperate effort to roll sideways and evaded the stamping hoofs by inches. The gelding lifted itself again and squealed with pain as a jagged piece of blazing timber dropped across its back. Somehow it bounded high, clearing Bellamy and, in its rage, tore through the curtain of flames into the open. Bellamy staggered to his feet and picked up the timber that had dropped on the gelding. Using its red-hot end as a prod he drove the remaining horses after the big gelding. All, that was, but his own mount. The roan was stamping about in wild-eyed terror. Bellamy had to approach the dancing hoofs with caution before grabbing at the head-rope. There was no time for soothing words. Twice, he led the animal towards the flame-barred doorway while almost every stitch of his clothing smouldered. Then the roan took the plunge and the pair rocketed into the safety of the street.

Outside, someone drenched him with a bucket of water. He turned to look at the buildings and saw that they were beyond all hope of being saved.

He remembered Holden and grabbed at the nearest man.

'Holden — ' he gasped. 'Did anyone get him out?'

The man was Red Malone. He took his time answering, and Bellamy was conscious of the fact.

'Sure, Holden's OK. Came out through the window.'

Bellamy said: 'Good,' and quite suddenly became aware of a score of hurts.

He glanced down at himself and saw that he was as near naked as mattered and what clothes were still sticking to him were mere charred remnants. He glanced at Malone. Something was wrong in the fact that the two were standing talking. He moved away stiffly and awkwardly, saw in the ruddy light of the dancing flames a score of half-dressed men vainly throwing buckets of water on to the fire.

Someone dashed up to him and asked if he were all right, and when he said he was, went rushing away, clanking bucket in hand. He was almost at the steps of the hotel when he knew what it was that had been wrong when he had stood with Malone.

Malone was fully dressed, even to his hat and bandanna. More than that — there had come from him a reek of kerosene and not warm kerosene either.

Bellamy sat down on the steps of the hotel. He felt tired beyond endurance. The shouts of the men down by the fire came to him as from a great distance. He closed his eyes and strove to fight again the waves of pain that now began to rack his entire body. How long he sat there humped in the shadows of the place he did not know but he was that way when a soft voice said:

'Are you hurt bad, Jeff?'

He knew it was Susan Moss without looking up. 'Not bad, I guess, Susan. I'll get up to my room now.'

'You'll come along to our place, if you can walk that far.'

Susan's voice was still soft, but it seemed to him very firm.

He said: 'OK, Susan,' and got groggily to his feet. It seemed a long way to the Moss's shack.

Sam Moss, still house-bound, looked at Bellamy with consternation.

'Holy cats, Jeff looks 'most burned to death. Here, feller, get sat down. Susan an' me'll fix you some, but I guess we'd better call the doc as well.'

'No,' Bellamy insisted. 'I'm scorched a little but I'll get over it.'

Susan brought oil and clean rags and scissors to cut away the scorched clothing, also a blanket to cover him. Bellamy had as bad a time as he could remember but went through it with scarcely a grunt. When he was bandaged and padded to Susan's satisfaction, Sam poured a man-sized glass of whiskey. Bellamy took most of it in one gulp then managed a grin.

'I guess I'll be all right now, an' thanks for the help. Guess I'll have to go an' get something that looks like clothes. Mind if I borrow this blanket to get over to the hotel?'

Susan shook her head determinedly. 'You're not going out like that.'

'It's plenty dark an' I'll be across the street in a few minutes.'

'I'm not thinking about the way you look. Jeff, you've been jumped more than once. How would you manage if someone tried to jump you when you couldn't get at your guns?'

'Sensible girl, ain't she?' grinned Sam. 'I guess she's right. You can stay here 'til morning then Susan can go across an' get the clerk to go into your room an' get some fresh clothes.'

Watching Susan's face, Bellamy felt compelled to blurt out: 'Susan don't need to ask the clerk. She knows her way to my room.'

Sam Moss's geniality vanished. 'What's that you say?'

Bellamy found himself wishing he had never spoken but there was no drawing back now. In any case he had to find out sometime why Susan had been in his room. Nevertheless —

Susan said in a strained voice: 'Jeff found me searching his room.'

Sam Moss seemed to shrink and draw within himself. It was a long time before he spoke, then the words came slowly.

'I always knew it'd catch up with me an' now it has. Soon as I saw you, Bellamy, I guessed you were from the County Office. I wanted to make sure. Susan knew that. That's why she searched your room, lookin' for your badge or some other proof, I suppose. Was that it, Susan?'

Bellamy cut in sharply: 'Here, hold your hosses, Sam. I don't come from no

County Office — or any other office.'

'What are you then, Jeff Bellamy?'

Susan's usually gentle voice had a surprising edge to it.

Bellamy gave a hitch to the blanket round his shoulders. 'Would it make any difference if you knew?'

Susan regarded him steadily. 'If I found a county badge in your war-sack or anywhere else, I'd have shot you. In the back if I couldn't do it any other way.'

Bellamy whistled. 'Looks like I come near to bein' a corpse. Well, as I said, I'm not from the county. I'm just a feller that came ridin' this way an' found trouble. So whatever you've done, Sam, it don't matter a hoot to me — providin' it weren't done recent.'

Time enough to tell Sam the real reason for his being in Red Rock when he knew him better, and he did not, for a moment, associate him with the death of Carl Dorlen.

'It weren't done recent,' Sam said steadily. 'I'll tell you about it. It was — '

Bellamy cut him off sharply. 'No.

'Sides, I'm plumb tired. I'd sure like to stretch out somewheres.'

Susan's hardness vanished immediately. 'I'll get blankets and a mattress.' She went quickly into another room.

Later, as comfortable as his numerous burns allowed, Bellamy drifted into an uneasy sleep telling himself that Sam's past was none of his business. There were things he himself had done in the stresses and hatreds of war that he wished he could forget.

Mid-morning found Bellamy leaning against Kerney's bar occasionally shifting to a different position to ease one or other of his burns.

Kerney, who had served him with the whiskey he was now drinking, said:

'You sure look kind of odd with most of your eyebrows missing, Bellamy.'

'I guess so. I ain't worried about that over much. What's eating me at the minute is, I've lost a good job.'

Kerney grinned. 'Feller like you can easily pick up another job.'

'Yeah — nursin' cows or somethin'.

That ain't much in my line. Matter of fact, I hate anythin' regular.'

'Here's Holden coming in.' Kerney filled another glass.

Holden took the glass in silence, swallowed the liquor in one gulp and pushed the glass back to Kerney.

'Fill it up. I want to get good and drunk.'

Kerney nodded. 'Sure, we know how you feel.'

Bellamy took in Holden's appearance. The man seemed to have aged ten years overnight. Obviously, he was just at the end of his endurance.

More to show his sympathy than for any other reason. Bellamy said:

'What you goin' to do now, Holden?'

Holden tossed back the second glass of whiskey. 'Do? What the hell is there for me to do except clear out? I'm finished — finished, I tell you, and by some lousy skunk I don't even know the name of.'

Kerney fiddled with his massive watch chain. 'Holden — you've made a good fight. I'd like to back you up — '

'Back me up!' Holden laughed harshly. 'There isn't anything to back up. I haven't got a thing left on wheels and anyone can have the horses for what they'd like to offer.'

'You still own the land,' Kerney persisted.

Bellamy glanced at Kerney. It struck him that the small piece of land that Holden's stage buildings had occupied could not be worth very much. Kerney read the question in Bellamy's glance.

'Holden owns every bit of land the town stands on.'

'And a hell of a lot it's worth,' Holden growled, 'at the rents I charge.'

Bellamy said thoughtfully: 'Seems to me it'll be worth a dern sight less if someone don't keep a stage line goin'.'

Kerney fished out cigars and handed them to the other two men. 'That's just the way I figure it. If Holden pulls out and no one else gets the line going again, this place'll be a ghost town in three months.'

'Wells Fargo'll chip in,' Holden grunted.

Bellamy shook his head. 'They won't. Wells Fargo is through with pioneering lines through bad country. They wouldn't offer you a nickel for the line now.'

'There you are, then. Like I said, I'm through.'

Kerney gave a despairing heave of his massive shoulders.

'Well, I guess that puts me out as well. No stage line, no town. I might as well close up any time.' He seemed lost in thought for a while, then said: 'I hate giving up without a fight though. Tell you what, Holden. I'll make you an offer for the lot. Land, stage line, horses — everything.'

Holden stared into space for a while. Bellamy read the struggle going on in the man's mind. Finally, Holden said: 'It's a deal, Kerney, though I'm damned if I don't feel like I'm selling you a salted claim.'

Kerney waved a fat hand. 'I'm sticking my own neck out. Let's drink on it. We can settle the details later.'

Bellamy left the two men talking.

Kerney had said nothing about wanting his help to reopen the stage line, so there would no longer be an excuse for hanging about Red Rock. He did not see how Kerney was going to make a go of it where Holden had failed, yet if he didn't, Red Rock would certainly become a ghost town like others that made small marks on the vast landscape; places of tenantless buildings with the clapboards falling off and the inside slowly filling up with sand and wind-blown debris, becoming by night coyote-haunted outposts. He gave a slight shiver. Red Rock was no picture town but at least it was a place of human habitation. Come to think of it, though Red Rock had sprung up in an odd place, fringed as it was to the North with near desert and to the South with poor quality range land, it might have been a mining town if it had been farther north. As it was, it was the sorriest kind of cow town with only a few small ranches centering upon it.

He idled time on the veranda of the

saloon watching the few men and women in the street. What would they do if Kerney failed to make a go of it? Pull out one at a time, he supposed. But where to and by what means? Many of them did not own so much as a single horse. For the most part they were content to scratch a living from the barren soil, the men eking out as extra hands on some distant ranches at round-up time.

He gave a mental shrug. It was hard, but lots of things were hard and he did not see what more he could do.

But it nagged him that still no one had even mentioned Dorlen or his death. It could be that it really had been an accident — a matter soon forgotten. On the other hand, there was the letter that had brought himself to Red Rock. Dorlen was dead, and Holden had trouble in plenty. He might just as well pull out.

The sight of Malone, with Lawson and Smith drifting towards the saloon brought him a sudden hot rage. He straightened up, the notion to pick a quarrel with the three, strong in his mind.

The men clattered up the steps giving him a casual nod before breasting open the batwings. Bellamy waited a few seconds, intending that they should get settled at the bar before he followed them in. As he moved toward the batwings, Holden came out. He looked a little more cheerful. Bellamy concluded that he had made the deal with Kerney satisfactorily.

Holden nodded to him and passed off the veranda. Bellamy walked inside and planted himself close beside Malone. Malone eased himself away a few inches.

'You're takin' plenty of space.' Bellamy's tone was deliberately offensive.

Malone glanced at him and moved a good two feet further along the bar, the other two men side-stepping at the same time.

Bellamy felt the anger in him dying. He tried to rekindle it by thinking of the dozen or so raw spots the fire had burned on him. Forcing a fight on a man was something he had never done before and he knew that if he succeeded in making Malone grab for his gun he would hate himself for it. Nevertheless, he said:

'Malone, you smell worse'n a skunk. Come to think of it, you stink of kerosene — the stuff they uses to start fires.'

Malone's dark face convulsed with suppressed rage. The knuckles of his clenched hands showed white but he made no move.

Bellamy stared at the man for a few moments then turned away, disgusted more with himself than with Malone. He stepped into the street and walked the few yards to the hotel. In his room he rammed gear together determined to leave the place right away instead of waiting until he was more fit to travel. He came downstairs, paid his score at the desk and, crossing the street to where his own mount had temporary stabling, met up with Susan Moss. She glanced at the bundles he was carrying.

'So you're pulling out?'

'That's right. Ain't nothing to stop here for now.'

'I suppose not. I think you should have stayed until those burns healed though.' She held out her hand to him. 'Well, goodbye, Jeff. It — it's been nice knowing you.'

He shook her hand. 'Sure, Susan, been nice for me.'

He watched for a few seconds as she crossed with quick steps to the store. Suddenly, he darted after her and caught her by the arm. It might be no business of his, but he owed something to her and Sam. She lifted her face, her puzzled eyes looking straight into his.

'Have you forgotten something, Jeff?'

'I reckon so. Forgot to pay a debt.'

He drew her away from the store and the few women who watched with curious eyes. He outlined the probable developments now that the stage line was out of action and the property changing ownership.

'Kerney won't make any better go of it than Holden,' he concluded. 'You an' Sam ought to pull out.'

'Pull out?' Susan looked troubled. 'But we can't.'

Bellamy shifted uncomfortably. 'Susan, you've got to. Everyone'll have to. Don't you see — Red Rock'll be a ghost town in no time.'

Susan turned away from him and almost ran toward the store. She flung a last word at Bellamy.

'We can't go, I tell you.'

Bellamy gave a shrug of his shoulders and moved in the direction of the stable again. He stopped in his lengthy stride, stood undecided for a moment then walked quickly up the street to Sam Moss's frame-house shack.

He was waiting at the picket fence gate when Susan came back from the store.

'Want to talk to you an' Sam,' he mumbled.

Susan nodded dumbly and led the way inside.

An hour later Bellamy came out of the shack with something near a scowl on his face. It had come to him unwanted that although there now seemed no possible solution to the trouble that had brought him to Red Rock he still had responsibilities in the place. Sam and Susan were friends of his now, without the means to leave the place, even if they had been willing to go. Others in the town were in a similar plight.

Bellamy stamped back into the hotel and threw his gear down. When the clerk asked nervously how long he intended to stay, Bellamy said:

'For ever, I guess, if it's any of your derned business.'

5

Kerney had a satisfied smile on his broad, fat face. Leaning on the end of his bar as he usually did puffing at a thick, black cigar and twiddling with his heavy gold watch chain, he oozed geniality. Even though the amount of business the saloon was doing would scarcely cover the cost of kerosene for the many lamps that were lit and he had twice observed the barkeep feed himself a free drink, Kerney did not cease to smile.

Somewhere round ten o'clock Kerney moved his vast figure from the bar and went into his little back office. There he pored over a large map. A map of the town and the trails leading to it. Staring at the map seemed to give him even greater satisfaction. The satisfaction of a man looking at the plans of some newly acquired property. Or at least as good as acquired. He had agreed on a figure for the purchase that Holden himself thought very generous under the circumstances. But as he had told Holden, he was a careful man who wanted everything about a transaction of this size to be in good legal order, and the deal would not be complete until both men had met and signed a deed to be drawn up by a lawyer in Durango.

Holden and himself were starting for Durango in the morning. There was no secret about the affair. Bellamy, who had met with and talked to Holden, knew about it when, at nearly eleven o'clock, Bellamy walked into the saloon. Bellamy even knew the amount of cash that would change hands. He thought Kerney was either very generous or just plumb foolish. Then just as Bellamy was ordering his drink he caught a glimpse of Red Malone in a mirror, coming, apparently towards the bar. Bellamy's mind registered this vaguely, then as the swamper handed a glass to him he wondered where Malone had come from.

Obviously, from Kerney's office. Something seemed wrong in that. Malone's reflection had now passed out of view of the mirror. That should have brought him to the bar but a glance to either side showed no sign of Malone. Bellamy picked up his glass, swung round in a casual manner to get a view of the rest of the room and assured himself that Malone was not in the place. Lawson and Smith were at the further end of the counter but Malone had evidently gone outside. Bellamy drank without haste, set down the glass and, with a nod to the barkeep made his own way outside.

There he stood for a few minutes on the veranda, accustoming his eyes to the velvet blackness of the night. At the same time he listened intently for noises that did not come from the saloon. Presently he caught the soft, clop of hoofs on the dirt road and instantly sidled along to the end of the veranda. He took the low rail in a bound and landed, soft-footed, at the side of the building. A few seconds later a rider showed as a blurred silhouette.

Bellamy had to guess that the rider was Malone, and as soon as the man was out of sight he darted across to the stable and, in less than five minutes, came out again astride the big roan.

He might, he thought, be on a wrong trail but Malone was more than a suspect character since the night of the fire, and whatever reason had sent him riding out of town at this hour should be worth looking into. Of a purpose he held the roan into a walk although, after so little exercise, the animal was more than anxious to break into a gallop.

Clear of the town he let the roan have its head and the big horse settled down to a long, raking stride that ate up the miles. With the first of the stage halts in sight he again reined in to a slow walk, confident that, by now Malone could not have much of a lead, and wary in case he had halted at this stage for some purpose. As no light streaks showed from the shuttered windows

Bellamy gave his mount free rein again. Coming to clear ground he caught sight of a shadowy figure perhaps a quarter of a mile ahead. He kept the rider just in view until horse and man seemed to merge into the blurred hump that was Zeke's place.

Bellamy swung aside from the trail and left his mount with trailing reins. He was still a few hundred yards from Zeke's shack when a light flared yellow streaks through the cracks of a shutter. Bellamy increased his pace until he could clearly discern the outline of the building. Suddenly a wide swathe of light cut the blackness of the night as a door opened. Almost on the instant of the light's glare came the startling roar of a six-gun and the accompanying red flash. Bellamy took it on the run, fired once at a dimly seen figure then, as a rider cleared from the deeper shadows of the buildings at a flying gallop, set his fingers to his lips in a shrill, piercing whistle. The roan responded instantly, coming to him head high to clear the trailing reins. Bellamy picked up the reins and bounded into the saddle.

Passing the open door of Zeke's shack he had a glimpse of a man lying on the ground and the wrappered form of Dolly bending over it. He had little doubt that the man on the ground was Zeke, just as he was nearly certain that the fast flying shadow ahead of him was Malone.

In two miles of mad galloping the big roan brought Bellamy within six-gun range of the man. He jerked out a Colt and thumbed back the hammer, changed his mind and holstered the weapon again. Malone, if it were he, would be more valuable alive. Another few minutes and he was almost within roping distance. Bending over the roan's neck he urged it to greater efforts.

The man ahead turned in the saddle, a gun flashed and roared, the slug singing close to Bellamy's head. Two more shots sang by high and wide and then Bellamy was clawing Malone from the saddle, trying at the same time to wrest the gun from his grip. The two horses bumped heavily together then, both thrown out of their stride, floundered widely apart. Bellamy, an arm locked around Malone, felt himself leaving the saddle. Too late he tried to recover his balance and went thudding to the ground dragging Malone on top of him. The breath knocked out of him, Bellamy still clung to Malone. Malone, on his part, had fallen fairly soft. More, he had retained his grip on his six-gun. He fired at almost point blank range but Bellamy, fighting and writhing to come to the top, upset his aim. Before Malone could trigger off another shot Bellamy's knee had doubled and thrust out with terrific force. Malone described an arc through the air and landed on his back. Bellamy's coming to his feet was like a volcanic eruption. So also were the twin blasts from his guns as the balls of his feet hit the ground. The slugs caught Malone in the act of rising, and the driving lead lifted him. He was dead when his body hit the earth again.

Sure of his aim Bellamy holstered his guns and went and stood over Malone's body. He looked at it with but one regret. He should have made Malone talk before he killed him.

Dolly was still at the door of the shack when Bellamy rode slowly up to it trailing Malone's horse with Malone's body over the saddle. Bellamy's glance went from her to the lifeless figure of Zeke.

'I'm derned sorry I didn't act a mite sooner,' he said. ''Course, I didn't know what Malone was up to.'

Dolly pulled the thin wrap tighter round her body. The movement seemed, to Bellamy, almost a shrug.

'So it was Malone that done it. I shoulda guessed it'd be that louse.'

Bellamy hitched the two mounts. 'I'll lift Zeke inside.'

This time the shrug was plain. 'Sure, I guess someone'll have to do it.'

Bellamy bent down and heaved the form of Zeke across one shoulder.

'Where'll I put him?'

'There's a spare bedroom. I'll light the lamp.'

Bellamy followed her into a room that contained four iron bedsteads. There were wafer thin mattresses but no blankets. Bellamy guessed, as he straightened Zeke's body on one of the beds, that the room was kept for occasional overnight passengers forced to stop there when the trail conditions were too bad. Coming out of the room he watched Dolly's face. There was certainly no sign of sorrow in it. In fact she didn't seem upset in the least by the sudden and violent death of her husband.

She caught his glance upon her and stared back at him. 'I'll make us some coffee.'

'Sure, I always drink coffee after a killin' and a murder.'

'Yeah, your sort would.'

She passed into the kitchen without further comment and came back some minutes later with a pot of coffee and two mugs.

'He weren't any good to me, you know. Too dern jealous. Knocked me about some too. Not that he had it all his own way. I could manage if I found something handy to slam him with.'

Bellamy took the mug of coffee she handed to him. Dolly knew plenty, he was sure. The thing was, would she talk? She wasn't the type to scare easily, that was certain. He decided to play it clever.

''Tain't no job for the marshal, that's one thing. Zeke's dead an' Malone, the man who shot him, is also.'

'The marshal? Him!' Dolly's voice was full of contempt.

Bellamy took a long drink of the coffee. 'How long's he been marshal?'

''Bout six months, I guess. Took the job after Anderson — the feller before him — fell off his hoss an' broke his neck.'

'Fell off his horse, eh? Lots of guys fall off horses an' don't get killed.'

Dolly's mouth parted in a sarcastic smile. 'Yeah, fell off his hoss like I told you. Right in town with lots of folks lookin' on. So he weren't pushed, if that's what you're thinkin'. Tell you another thing, too. It ain't no use you tryin' to pump me for information. I don't know anythin' an' I wouldn't tell if I did.'

Bellamy set the mug down. 'You're lyin'. Any time I feel you ought to talk, there's ways of coaxin' you — and don't figure on your sex protectin' you too much. Just at present I don't feel called on to get rough with you.'

He swung out of the place and climbed into the saddle, not quite certain whether his threat had been a vain one or not.

Coming into town with Malone's body trailing on the horse behind him, he stopped outside the marshal's office. He guessed Hamble would be in bed, so beat on the door with the butt of a gun. Five minutes of intermittent hammerings brought no reply.

Bellamy grunted. Hamble missing. What business kept the marshal out of his bed, and who else in the town was doing a night prowl? He decided to try the saloon. After all, the stage line was now practically Kerney's business, so the murdering of Zeke would be Kerney's business also. It took five minutes of hammering on the doors of the saloon before an upstairs window shot open and Kerney's voice demanded to know what all the row was about.

Bellamy told him, then waited the few minutes it took Kerney to come downstairs and open up.

'Don't see what the devil you had to bring him here for,' were Kerney's first words on opening the door.

'Figured as the stage line is as good as yours, you'd want to know what was happening,' Bellamy answered briefly. 'Not only that, but there's Dolly Smethers out there alone — 'cept, of course, for Zeke's corpse.'

Kerney put a match to a lamp. Watching him as the light glowed on his face Bellamy thought he did not look like a man just roused from sleep. He registered the fact, storing it alongside the fact that Hamble was either not at home or had chosen not to answer the hammering on his door.

The lamp burning to his satisfaction, Kerney turned to face Bellamy.

'I reckon Dolly's the cause of this trouble. Maybe you've seen how she acts, giving the eye to almost every man who comes near the place, including Malone. I know Zeke's cut up rough about it more than once.'

It sounded like a good reason to Bellamy, except for one fact. Dolly had shown not the slightest emotion over the death of Malone. Another thing, Kerney had shown no curiosity as to how he himself had happened to be on the spot.

In apparent agreement with Kerney, he said: 'Yeah, I guess you could be right. Women like Dolly can sure cause a whole heap of trouble. What'd I better do with this Malone feller? Guess you wouldn't want him dumped here an' the horse'll get plumb tired if we don't lift him off pretty soon.'

'I'll help you lift him in here. I'll fix to have him buried in the morning and — '

Kerney got that far when the sound of horses pounding at a gallop interrupted him. With a movement surprisingly quick for a man of his bulk he jerked about and puffed out the light. Bellamy sprang towards the door at the same instant that half-a-dozen gunshots shattered the night silence. The first outbursts of shots were followed by more, and then, as Bellamy reached the door the roar of a shotgun added to the racket. He came rocketing out of the doorway with a gun in each hand. At the hitch rail the two horses were squealing and tugging to break free. Gun flashes seemed, at first, to show from all directions but in less than a second he understood that most of the shooting was being done in front of Banks's store. Dimly, he made out that five or six horsemen were cavorting about in front of the store and emptying their six-guns into the place as they wheeled about. The rest of the shooting was coming from various shacks and properties opposite the store.

Bellamy made for his own mount then almost in the act of vaulting into the saddle, changed his mind.

Riding down the street with the indignant citizens throwing lead at those in front of the store would be plain suicide. He yanked the rifle from the saddle-boot and set himself to the business of sighting on the dimly seen figures weaving and twisting about. In the uproar of violent explosions the sharp crack of the rifle made but little addition. But before the weapon was properly warmed in his hands the attacking gunmen left the place at a mad gallop. For some minutes after that, odd shots fired by men not yet convinced that the attackers had re- treated continued to explode. Then, by degrees, and to the accompaniment of much shouting and bawling, the shoot- ing ceased.

Bellamy reloaded the rifle and

pushed it back in its scabbard before walking down the street. By the time he got to the store a dozen or more half-dressed men were there. One of them called loudly for a lamp.

'They's a couple of the buzzards here on the ground. Bet I got one of 'em.'

Bellamy hung at the outskirts of the little crowd until Banks came out of the store carrying a hurricane lamp. Then he pushed his way forward and, in the yellow circle thrown by the lamp, saw two men stretched out. One was Hamble, the other, a man named Keven. Bellamy remembered seeing him about the town but knew little of him.

Someone said: 'Now we ain't got no marshal an' hell knows who'll take the job with all the trouble we got lately. One thing, no one can't say Hamble weren't doin' his job this time. Musta rode slap into it as soon as it started.'

Bellamy walked back toward the saloon without disclosing his thoughts, and certain in his mind that, if anyone took the trouble to dig the slugs out of the dead men, they would match up with the bore of his own rifle.

Kerney had lit lamps in the saloon when Bellamy walked in. Joe Sanger, the bartender, was hovering round, and Holden, half dressed, was talking nervously to Kerney. Bellamy heard Holden say:

'I tell you, Kerney, I'm scared to death of this town. I'm getting out, pronto. If you're still of a mind to go through with the deal we'll ride into Durango come sun-up, and I ain't coming back neither.'

Kerney appeared about to assent when he noticed the arrival of Bellamy.

Bellamy looked at the pair. 'You need a new town marshal.'

Kerney appeared startled. 'Hamble — dead? How did that happen?'

'Got in the way of a slug — one of mine I should guess from what I saw of the wound.'

'One of yours? How — '

Bellamy waited for Kerney to complete his sentence and when he did not, said in a flat voice:

'Some guys reckon Hamble must have rode in to break up the ruckus. Can't say, myself. Never saw the marshal in any kind of action before.'

'Sure, that'd be the way of it. Hamble heard the row and went straight into action like any marshal would.'

Kerney spoke the words rapidly as a man does when anxious to agree.

'OK then. That takes care of Hamble. There was another guy got it as well. Feller called Keven. Know anything about him?'

'Keven? He's just one of the men living near the end of the town. Likely he was helping Hamble.'

'Could be, I suppose. Well, that's the way of it. When shooting starts innocent men go down while the guilty buzzards get away with it.'

Kerney bit the end off a cigar. 'Yes, I guess it's often that way.'

Bellamy went on as if talking to himself: 'I wonder what it was all about? Seemed like they had a dead set on the store, but if they wanted to loot the store that weren't hardly the way to go about it. Reckon I'll go along and see Banks. Mebbe he's got some ideas on the subject.'

Halfway to the door Bellamy turned round. 'About the marshal's job. Who has the appointing of the new man?'

Kerney hesitated for a moment. 'Us bigger men, I guess. Myself, Holden, Banks and a few others. We pay the marshal's wages so we have the appointing. Of course, we let the rest of the folks have a say, but you know how it is.'

'Sure, the guy with the most dough has the loudest call. I was just thinking that, as there's no freight hauling to do and I could use a job — '

Holden cut in eagerly. 'I reckon you'd be the very man for the job, Bellamy.'

Bellamy allowed a slight smile to crease his features as he passed out to the street.

Down at the store he found that all but a few men had gone home again and the rest dawdled no longer when he himself arrived. Banks himself was plainly a very scared man, only too anxious to get inside and bar the door again.

Bellamy went inside with him. 'Thought I'd have a little talk with you seeing I stand a good chance of being the next town marshal.'

'Oh sure, sure. Kerney in favour of appointing you?'

'Holden's all for it and Kerney hasn't said anything against it. I reckon it depends on you a lot.'

'Mebbe, mebbe. Yes, I guess it does. Look, what do you make of this attack on my place tonight?'

'You keep any dough salted away here?'

'No, least, only a few bucks. Not enough to make it worthwhile stickin' the place up.'

Bellamy helped to bar the door. 'And if those skunks had gotten inside, there weren't very much they could have carried away on their horses.'

Banks agreed. 'That's so.' He turned a scared face toward Bellamy. 'Say, you don't think they were just out to murder *me*?'

'Either that or scare you into running out of town.'

'But I haven't done anything. Look, I don't believe I've made an enemy in the place all the years I've been here.'

Bellamy perched himself on a dry-goods box. ''Bout how long would that be?'

'How long? Cripes, that was away back in — Oh, I dunno. Place was a small digging camp then. Folks had high hopes too. All on account of a feller coming in to Dodge City with a chunk of rock bigger than your two fists that assayed higher than any rock we'd ever heard of. The feller died of some kind of fever. Had it when he hit the town. He didn't talk much but it was enough for me and some others to find our way here. 'Course, it turned out like a lot more places. A little pay dirt, about enough to keep a guy in beans, but no real bonanza.'

Bellamy nodded sympathetically. 'So you and the other guys decided to stay here and try to make a go of it in other ways.'

'Something like that, though I'm the only one of the original crowd who hoped to make a fortune. The others came when we'd got going a bit with cattle and such. Holden came and started a freight line, then I think it was Dorlen after him, or mebbe it was the other way round.'

'Dorlen. I don't seem to know him,' Bellamy bluffed.

'Shucks, I forgot about you being a newcomer. Dorlen had the saloon before Kerney took over. Dorlen fell down the trap into his own liquor cellar and broke his neck. Joe Sangers found him when he opened up in the morning.'

'Kind of a shock for Joe, coming out of his room and finding his boss dead, guess it comes hard if you've been with a guy for a long time.'

'Joe hadn't been there long, only a few weeks. Still it would be a shock — say you'll stay the night with me will you? I'm more than a mite scared and if you're going to be the new marshal — '

Bellamy smiled. 'Sure, I'll stay the night. You get bedded down as usual. Marshals do their sleepin' in the day time, anyway.'

Bellamy spent the remainder of the night hours thinking. Dorlen found with a broken neck. It might have been an accident but it could have been murder. Sangers was a newcomer arriving not long before Kerney. Suspicious maybe when tied up with the rather vague troubles mentioned in Dorlen's letter and the undoubted attacks first on Holden's stage business and then on the store. But what was behind it all?

6

Jeff Bellamy, Marshal of Red Rock. Smiling grimly at his new title and wondering just how long he would hold it, Bellamy unlocked the door of the shack the late marshal had called his office. Bellamy's purpose was not so much to use the place himself but to find out if his predecessor had left any papers that might give a clue to the various criminal happenings that had taken place in and around Red Rock. Almost on opening the door he sensed that he had been outwitted. The place was much too tidy. The battered and scarred table that served for a desk was clear of even the tiniest scrap of paper. In fact, it was even clear of dust. The single cupboard in the room was empty of everything. In the room at the back which contained a broken down iron bed and the heavy wooden barred door of the lock-up, the same evidence of tidiness existed. Bellamy came back into the office and lifted the lid off the stove. It was full of charred paper. He sat himself on the single chair and rolled himself a smoke.

It was not yet noon. Half an hour ago, at a meeting of a few men in the saloon, he had been offered, and had accepted, the post of marshal. Kerney himself had voiced the offer, and when he had made it, it sounded as if he genuinely wanted Bellamy to have the post. And on the face of it, it seemed to Kerney's advantage, as to everyone else's, to have a two-handed gun fighter as marshal of Red Rock. Bellamy did not forget, however, that he had practically nominated himself for the job. Neither did he figure that someone had been doing him a favour in so carefully cleaning up after Hamble.

Out in the street again Bellamy made his way towards Sam Moss's shack. Sam was sitting in the little porch and rose a little stiffly from his chair when

Bellamy approached.

'Sure glad to see you getting about again,' Bellamy said.

'Yeah. Be derned glad to be doin' some work again. I don't know what at though. What do you make of that business over at the store, Jeff?'

'Adds up like I told you before, Sam. Someone wants this town cleaning right out. Banks is the kind that scares pretty easy. If he was to quit town that, on top of the freight line being bust up, would make things mighty awkward for folks.'

Sam scratched the side of his grey head. 'Seems like you could be right but there don't seem no reason for it.'

Susan came in sight at that moment, walking in quick steps from the direction of the store.

Sam Moss chuckled. 'I reckon Susan figured I'd forget to take that pan off the stove for her.'

Bellamy touched his hat as Susan came near. 'Hello, Susan, what's all the hurry?'

'That Mr Kerney's getting impossible.

115

Just as I was coming past the saloon, old Mrs Cooney came along struggling with a great piece of charred lumber. She wanted it for stove wood. I was just going to help her to carry it when Mr Kerney came out on the veranda. At first he was all smiles and, 'Good morning, ladies,' then he spotted the lumber. Straight away his manner changed. He didn't even ask where Mrs Cooney had got the lumber, told her to quit rooting round in the debris of the freight office.'

'Did she get the lumber from Holden's old place?' Bellamy asked quietly.

'Yes. At least, I guess she did. There's nowhere else in town where she could have got charred lumber. I didn't half give Mr Kerney the length of my tongue, I can tell you. When I'd finished he said he was sorry but he just didn't want anyone poking round the place in case something heavy fell on them. Huh, men and their excuses.'

Still indignant, Susan flounced inside. Sam Moss grinned at Bellamy.

'Guess I'll have to drive pretty

straight for an hour or so now. She's proper burned up.'

Bellamy grinned back. 'Guess so, Sam. I'll be getting along and tend to my new job.'

He had intended probing Sam's knowledge of the town in its early days but this bit of information supplied by Susan had set his mind working in a new direction. Kerney getting het up about some old, charred lumber which, strictly speaking, was not yet his property, seemed to require a little thought. The saloon was as good a place as any in which to think so he made his way there.

Outside, two horses at the hitch rail distinguished themselves from the others by the fact that they carried behind their saddles the sort of rolled bundle that indicates a journey of more than one day's duration. Bellamy guessed the mounts were waiting for Holden and Kerney. Inside, the sight of the pair putting away a substantial meal confirmed his guess.

Holden seemed pleasantly excited. 'Well, this is it, Bellamy. Kerney and me made a deal and when it's fixed up legal I ain't coming back. I'm going to get me some quiet little place and settle down to doin' dam' all.'

'Hope you enjoy it,' Bellamy answered. 'Making a kind of late start though, aren't you? That is, if you two gents are figuring to ride into Durango.'

It was Kerney who answered: 'Stopping overnight at Zeke's place. I want to have a good look round the place for one thing and we'll get into Durango about noon of the following day, which is a handier time for seeing the lawyer.'

'We're taking four men with us in case of trouble,' Holden volunteered.

Bellamy nodded. 'Have yourself a good trip then.'

He crossed to the bar, bought himself a beer and stood drinking it thoughtfully. It seemed to him likely that the two men would get into Durango without incident. What he could not figure was, what Kerney's move would be after the sale had been made legal.

When the pair and their escort of four riders had cleared the street Bellamy walked down to the scene of the burnt-out freight office. He wanted to see if he could figure out why Kerney had been so angry over Mrs Cooney taking away the scorched piece of lumber. Looking at the blackened shambles it seemed as if there was little worth taking away, even for stove-wood. The charred ruins seemed to have fallen into two distinct sections. One lot nearly level with the ground, the other forming a distinct hump some four or five feet higher. He moved round the place trying to understand what had formed the humped up part, then remembered that the loading bay had a high platform to one side of it. A glance at the ground nearby showed him something not easily seen when the buildings had been standing. Taking a line right from the saloon, the ground at the back of the building lots rose steadily until here, where the freight office had been, it formed a small out-crop of rock. When Holden had had the place built he had taken advantage of this lump to make a loading bay of it.

Bellamy turned away from the place whistling a little tune. Going back up the street he got the roan out of the stable and cantered out of the town, then made a wide circle away from the trail in such a way as to bring him behind the site of the ruined freight office. Swinging the horse backwards and forwards as if he was exercising the animal he criss-crossed a five or six mile area of dusty, flat uninteresting ground. Ground that was practically featureless except for an occasional humped outcrop of grey rock. But here and there, and mostly close to some rock, shallow depressions, long since nearly levelled by natural forces, showed where men had been digging. Mute evidence of the disappointment of many a gold seeker. Bellamy returned to the town even more thoughtful.

In the late evening he called again on Sam Moss, enjoyed a pleasant meal served and cooked by Susan, and had a long yarn with Sam about the days when men would drop everything and journey a thousand miles at the mere hint of yet another gold-strike. Sam was very knowledgeable about rock formations and seam faults and Bellamy absorbed the information like a cactus soaks up water.

With the morning he purposed to ride out and see Dolly Smethers, having no particular reason for doing so except that he guessed Dolly knew something more than he himself did. He changed his mind, however, when in coming into the street he saw a newcomer riding in. Tall as himself, the stranger rode a deep-chested mare, near to coal black, and sported a pearl-handled six-gun in a holster having silver mountings. The silver trimmings were repeated on the man's spurs and round the band of his black Stetson.

Bellamy lounged on the saloon

veranda while the newcomer dismounted and looped the reins over the hitch-rail.

The man in the black hat moved in a leisurely fashion about the business of tethering his mount and did not lift his eyes towards Bellamy until the process was completed. Then he gave Bellamy a long, insolent stare, finally settling his eyes on Bellamy's badge.

'Huh — town marshal, I see.'

'That's right. Any objections?'

'Not so long as you don't get in my hair.'

Bellamy smiled thinly. 'Aiming to make trouble, are you? I haven't yet decided whether I'll let you stay in town. What's your name an' where do you come from?'

'Brown — an' I come from the last place I stopped at. See?'

Bellamy's smile remained the same. 'OK, Mr Brown — if that is your name, you can stay. And if you make any trouble I'll see your headboard has Brown printed on it.'

Bellamy turned his back deliberately and went back into the saloon. He reached the door when Brown called:

'Hey you — marshal. I reckon you've got a yellow streak clean up the middle of your back.'

Bellamy swung about, the smile still on his lips, but no longer in his eyes.

'Listen, feller. If you want to draw on me, do it now or any other time you like. You don't have to bother about trying to raise my dander, an' the only reason you're still on your feet is, I want to find out for certain who sent you here. Now either pull that gun of yours or quit trying to razz me.'

Brown stared at him for a while then dropped his eyes. 'Guess I was only trying to take you for a walk.'

Bellamy said pleasantly: 'You're a dern, tootin' liar. You figured if I lost my temper I wouldn't be so handy on the draw. I'm warning you, Brown, get out of town before I come looking for you.'

Again, Bellamy turned his back

deliberately and this time went to follow him. Lounging with his back against the bar he could see the hat and the top of Brown's head as the man moved down the street. Curious to know what the next move would be, he spent some time assessing Brown's possibilities.

The man looked a killer. Sent, no doubt, to take care of himself. There was little else to account for the man's appearance in town.

Bellamy had got that far in his thinking when a series of six-gun shots sounded. He moved outside quickly and saw that Brown was using the sign over the store for target practise, to the obvious fright of several people running away from the store.

Bellamy's lips compressed into a thin line. Brown was taking a peculiar way in which to force a fight. A drunken cowpoke carrying on in the same manner could have been slugged from behind and disarmed. Brown was not drunk and had chosen a sure way to beat himself to a draw.

Stepping down to the street Bellamy walked towards Brown. While he was covering the distance Brown pumped out empty shells and reloaded with a speed Bellamy was compelled to admire. Brown raised the gun for further target work and at the same time turned his head so that his gaze fell on Bellamy.

'Stop that, Brown,' Bellamy called in level tones. 'I don't allow shootin' in the street.'

Brown regarded him insolently. '*You* don't allow shootin' in the street. An' who the hell are you, Mister two-gun marshal?'

Bellamy's continued walking had brought him to within a few feet of Brown.

'Holster that gun, Brown or I'll beat your brains out with it.' As he spoke the words Bellamy seemed about to turn to one side.

Brown gave a sarcastic grin and came round on his feet to suit the altered angle. 'Oh yeah — ' he began.

Bellamy chose that moment to dive straight at Brown's ankles. Brown's gun roared immediately, the flame scorching the back of Bellamy's neck.

Together, the pair went down in the dust, Bellamy still retaining his grip on Brown's ankles, who was almost on top of him. Bellamy lost no time in squirming round and planting a vicious knee jab in Brown's belly. Brown howled with pain and lost his hold on the gun. Bellamy came to his feet like a spring uncoiled, swept up the gun and whipped it viciously across Brown's face as he tried to rise. Brown went staggering and blood rushed from a wide gash in his cheek. Bellamy hit him twice more with the gun then tossed the weapon far down the street. Brown swayed drunkenly, his face streaming blood.

Bellamy said harshly. 'You've got 'til sundown to get out of town. If you're here after that, I'll do the target practise.'

He turned away and, without a further glance at Brown, walked with slow strides towards the hotel. There, recalling his earlier intention to talk to Dolly Smethers, he cleaned himself up then took the trail. He arrived at the place in the mid-afternoon and unsaddled and stabled the roan without seeing any sign of Dolly. Walking into the shack, however, it was plain that she knew of his arrival. A table was set for a meal and Dolly herself looked as if she had just smartened herself up. She gave him a brittle smile.

'Hello there, feller. Come to make me talk?'

Bellamy grinned. There was something behind Dolly's brash front that he liked. 'Let's get some of this trail dirt off then you can listen to me talk.'

'Sure, that'll be just dandy.' She poured water in a tin basin and handed him a rough towel. 'It'll have to be beans. We ain't seen much else since the stage line quit.'

Bellamy started sluicing. 'OK, beans it is.'

She hovered about while he towelled

himself and then set beans with a microscopic piece of bacon before him. Bellamy made no comment until he had eaten and she had poured coffee, then he said:

'What do you aim to do, Dolly?'

'Me — without Zeke you mean? Oh, I guess I can carry on all right, tending stage hosses is somethin' I can manage OK. Did it often enough when Zeke was here.'

Bellamy fished out tobacco and papers. 'Suppose there aren't any stage horses to look after.'

'Don't be crazy. There just has to be a stage, or at least a freight line. Red Rock'd just die without one.'

'Yeah, I know. How about if someone wanted just that to happen?'

'That's plumb foolish talk, I — ' Suddenly her face went pale. 'It's not true, is it? You're lying to me, tryin' to make me talk like you said you would.'

Bellamy shook his head. 'I'm not dead certain, but I'm not stringing you along.'

Distrust, fear and desperation chased each other across Dolly's face. Finally she said:

'OK, I'll tell you what I know. Mind, I'm not supposed to know anythin' but Zeke was never clever enough to hide anythin' from me. Kerney planned to run Holden out of business an' run the line himself. Reckoned there was a lot of profit in it.'

'So you didn't actually have anything to do with it yourself? Didn't slice that tug line for instance?'

Anger flashed on Dolly's face. 'You saw what Zeke done to my face, didn't you? That was for tryin' to ride after you an' tell you about it.'

Bellamy smiled. 'Sorry, Dolly, but I had to be certain. Now, this is the way I figure it. Kerney's managed to squeeze Holden out all right. Done it nicely. Holden even feels grateful to him. But Kerney isn't going to run that line any more. He wants Red Rock to die.'

'That's crazy. Why'd he want to do that?'

'Tell you when I'm more certain. Thanks for checking my suspicions on Kerney. Meantime, hold on if you can. I reckon the stage line'll run again, even if I have to run it myself.' He rose from the table. 'I'll be getting back now.'

'It'll be plumb dark before you get half way there, an' your hoss'll be most tuckered out. So will you, for that matter. Why not stay the night?'

Bellamy grinned. 'You forget, I'm marshal of Red Rock.'

'Damn you, if I'd thought you'd run out on me I wouldn't have talked.'

Bellamy walked to the door. 'Dolly, you don't fool me any. You've told me only half the truth. The half I already knows.'

It was pitch dark when Bellamy rode into Red Rock. A sliver of moon chased through thin wisps of cloud and made the street a place of sliding shadows alternating with pale streaks of half light. Bellamy put away a horse as weary as himself then crossed the street to the hotel. With one foot almost on the bottom step he halted.

Suddenly, all the dropping weariness went from his limbs and he was as alert as a colt that has sensed the nearness of a snake. A moment later a voice he recognized as belonging to Brown said softly:

'OK, marshal. Turn round and have it in the front.'

Bellamy did not move a muscle. 'Shoot if you want to. If I've got to be killed by a snake I might as well have snake marks on me.'

Brown laughed softly then came the slight click of the Colt's hammer being thumbed back. Bellamy's spine went rigid as he waited for the blast. Then the shattering roar of a shotgun split the night silence. In spite of his self-control Bellamy jumped, but before he could act the shot-gun roared again. Then came two loud reports from a six-gun. Bellamy flattened to the side of the veranda, at the same time dragging at his own gun. The six-gun that had fired before belched flame from behind the angle of the saloon but there was no answering fire.

Bellamy uttered a prayer of thanks to whoever had blasted off with a shotgun and sent Brown scampering to the side of the saloon. He got himself to a crouching position, pulled his left hand Colt and sent slugs from both guns to the corner of woodwork which covered Brown. He followed up with a run that sent him hurtling down the space between the saloon at breakneck speed and rounded the next corner to come behind Brown with both guns blazing. Brown fired once in reply, found the position untenable and bolted for the street. Bellamy came pounding after him and reached the street just in time to see Brown disappear between two shacks on the opposite side. Bellamy pulled up short and hugged the shadows cast by the saloon. In his view the fate of Brown was sealed. The man could not get far from town without his horse and that horse was in the next stall to Bellamy's own mount. The stable door was right opposite to Bellamy and was now bathed in soft moonlight.

After a little waiting and listening Bellamy planted himself on the saloon veranda and settled down to wait. His guns reloaded and holstered he checked patiently on the sounds that belonged to the night. The soft swish of the breeze over the roof tops, the occasional slap of a loose clapboard, the chirrup of a grasshopper suddenly starting and as suddenly ceasing. Then a long silence when the breeze died for a while, the silence followed by the hoarse chanting of a bullfrog. That also ceased, then, startingly clear to his ears came the sound of a boot against stone. Brown was moving after almost an hour of silence. Bellamy waited almost another hour during which the passage of the moon sliding across the sky moved the soft light from the stable door, leaving it in purple shadow.

Watching the shadow, Bellamy rose silently to his feet as the depth of its colouring changed slowly at one side. He waited another ten seconds then his right hand gun came sliding softly from its holster. He called out softly: 'Brown, make your draw. Your last.'

In the half minute of silence that followed he watched the changing depth of the shadow, then thumbed back the hammer of the Colt. Close upon the click of the hammer came a scurry of sounds from across the street, then the startling flash and roar of Brown's gun.

Bellamy went down in a dive, his left hand fanning the Colt. Three more gun flashes threw red and orange light across the stable door, then in the silence the breeze took up its gentle sighing.

Bellamy stepped down from the veranda, crossed the short distance to the hotel and went inside. The clerk, wide awake for once, stared at him with scared eyes.

Bellamy said: 'That feller, Brown. I guess he won't be checking in tonight.'

7

Kerney climbed from the saddle and beat the trail dust from his garments. He was stiff and sore from the long ride, nevertheless, his heavily jowled face expressed the utmost satisfaction. His four-arm bodyguard followed him as he stumped into the saloon, satisfaction showing on their faces also. With the coming of the sunset the lamps had been lighted in the saloon and the glow of yellow light with its promise of a long drink was a cheering sight to the five, dust-choked men. The five made instantly for the bar, then suddenly checked themselves.

Bellamy, leaning at the far end of the bar, gave a wave of his hand.

'Howdy, fellers. Dry work I reckon. Have the first on me.'

Kerney was the first to recover his poise. 'Nonsense, Bellamy, the drinks

135

are on me. Set 'em up, Joe.'

'Good trip? Everything OK?' Bellamy asked casually.

Kerney swallowed thirstily before answering.

'Sure, everything's OK. Holden's figuring on taking a little place about thirty mile the other side of Durango. Rode out to see it almost as soon as we'd settled things.'

Bellamy noticed that Kerney's glance kept wandering about the saloon eyeing the other occupants of the place.

'Looking for someone?' Bellamy asked.

'Me? No, just thought there weren't many fellers in the place tonight.' Kerney put the glass to his lips again.

'Thought mebbe you were looking for a guy named Brown.'

Kerney choked on his drink, spluttered and became red in the face.

Bellamy clapped him on the back sympathetically.

'Went down the wrong way, eh? So did Brown. Coupla fellers helped me plant him this morning.'

Kerney, still coughing and spluttering choked out: 'I don't know what the hell you're talking about. Don't know any feller named Brown.'

'That's the name we buried him under.'

Bellamy swallowed his own drink and walked out of the saloon just as a burst of gunfire racketed through the street. He made a two-handed grab for his guns, then straightened up a little sheepishly. He had forgotten that today was the end of the month. Pay day on the scattered ranges and the only day in the month on which Red Rock came really alive. A bunch of yelling, whooping riders came tearing down the street to a sliding halt at the saloon hitch rail.

Bellamy met them with a friendly nod. 'Easy with the hardware, fellers.'

A tall youngster peered in the half light at his badge. 'Hey, fellers, get a look at the new marshal, packing two guns as well. How're yer, marshal?'

Bellamy gave him a friendly push towards the batwings. 'Go buy yourself a drink an' remember what I said about the shooting.'

As they trooped inside the saloon a second noisy bunch came whooping down the street and behind them, a single rider. Something about the single rider attracted Bellamy's attention. He seemed somehow to lack the carefree spirit that held all the other men. The man drew up to the hitch rail, glanced about him in an uncertain manner then climbed stiffly from the saddle.

Bellamy walked towards him. 'Howdy, feller.'

'Howdy, yourself. I'm looking for a guy named Bellamy.'

'Then you've sure found him. I'm Bellamy.'

'Jeff Bellamy?' the rider insisted.

'The same. There ain't no other Bellamy round here that I know of.'

The rider fished in his shirt pocket. 'Got a letter for you from Lin Jones. Lin reckons it's important.'

Bellamy took the letter. 'Better come over to what they call the marshal's office.'

He led the way across the street and unlocked the door of the office and put a match to the kerosene lamp.

In silence he read:

Dear Bellamy

I heard they had made you marshal of Red Rock, so I reckon you ought to know that Holden got his about an hour after Kerney and the other four left here. As far as I can make out Holden got into a fight in the street but no one seems quite clear what happened and the guy who shot him got clear away. Maybe it was just what it seems, maybe not. Anyway I thought you ought to know right away. Sim Pesketh, who brings this letter can be trusted with any message you want to send back.

Yours truly,
Lincoln Jones.

Bellamy looked at Sim Pesketh. 'Sim, I sure appreciate the tough ride you've had bringing this note from Lin. Seems to me it'll have to be another tough ride back. The way I figure it, poor Holden may have been murdered. If so, I'd like it so no one here guesses you brought any message.'

Sim nodded. 'I could double right back and put up at the first stage halt.'

'I got a better idea. You stay here for the night. I'll fix your horse in the lean-to at the back. Then you can be away before dawn without having to call in at any stage halts. It's kinda tough on you and the horse, but — '

'It's OK by me. I knew Holden an' liked him plenty. Any message for Lin?'

'Yeah. Ask him to try and find out if Holden got a cheque for the deal he made with Kerney an' whether he got it into the bank or not. Now I'll fix your horse an' get you some grub an' such.'

Bellamy did what he had promised then made his way back to the saloon. It might be as well, he thought, if he acted the part of town marshal. He only hoped none of the cowpokes would act up enough to warrant being slung in the lock-up. That would be more than awkward.

In the saloon the din was hideous. Besides the twenty or so range hands every other man in the town seemed to have crowded in and the pressure up against the bar was almost as great as in the centre of a herd of steers. Bellamy frowned. The range hands had been in town for little more than an hour and already several were almost saturated with liquor. Quite a few more were argumentatively drunk. Kerney, he noticed, had put two extra men behind the bar and they were filling glasses as fast as they could go.

Pushing his way nearer the counter Bellamy broke up the beginnings of a fight, quelling the two belligerents with a cold, hard stare. Then a youngster grabbed him by the arm.

'Hey, marshal, feed yourself a drink. You don't havta pay. Red-eye, suds, gin, it's all the same. Here, have mine, I'll get me another.'

He tried to push a slopping glass into Bellamy's hand but Bellamy thrust him to one side and using his elbow freely, ploughed a way to the bar. The youngster had not exaggerated. Joe Sangers and two helpers were handing out whatever was asked for without bothering about the till. Kerney, at the far end of the bar, removed a cigar from his teeth to grin widely at him. Sangers pushed a large glass of red-eye towards him but Bellamy ignored it and bawled above the din.

'Hey, Kerney, I want to talk to you.'

Kerney moved ponderously down the other side of the bar, 'Well — marshal?'

Bellamy's mouth tightened. 'What's the idea of all this?'

Kerney smirked. 'Just standing treat to the boys. I reckon I've made a good deal with Holden and these boys have been good customers of mine. No law against standing a treat is there?'

He made to move away but Bellamy

shot a hand out and held him.

'No law as far as I know, Kerney. I haven't made one yet. Maybe I'll get round to it soon. Maybe I'll get around to some other law making at the same time.'

Kerney scowled at him. 'I'd like to see you make that law against free liquor right now, Bellamy. I reckon even those two guns of yours wouldn't be enough to enforce it.' He shook himself free of Bellamy's hold. 'Try it and see.'

Bellamy smiled thinly. 'OK, start a ruckus if you're set on the idea. You win for the moment but it's the last hand that counts in this game.' He pushed back from the bar and went outside again.

Kerney had started something that was going to be mighty hard to keep in control. After a moment's thought Bellamy made his way to Seth Cavan's place. Seth had put on a nearly clean apron and had his cook stove almost red hot in anticipation of the boys crowding in for eats.

Bellamy said: 'Better get up your shutters, Seth. The boys are unusually high tonight. In fact if you take my advice, you'll close up altogether.'

Cavan stared at him. 'Close up on pay night! Gosh, dern it, Jeff, it's the only time a guy makes a bit of dough.'

Bellamy shrugged. 'Well, I've warned you. I don't reckon I can hold them down without killing half-a-dozen, an' I won't be doin' that.'

He moved on to the store. Banks also expected to do extra business with the boys. Banks took the warning seriously and scuttled round like a frightened hen, moving stock to a back room and getting up shutters. Bellamy moved across the street calling on shacks where he knew there were children or ageing women, warning them to stay indoors whatever racket they heard from the street. His last call was at Sam Moss's house. Both Sam and Susan were just about ready to go to bed but Susan opened the door and asked him in.

Sam listened to what he had to say in silence, then said: 'That's sure a poisonous trick, feeding those boys free liquor, and gin and red-eye at that.'

Bellamy noticed Sam's eyes staring to the shotgun hanging on two nails on the wall.

'You won't need that, Sam, I promise.'

Susan gave a gasp of relief. 'Thank goodness for that.'

Bellamy moved towards the door, then paused.

'Say, someone used a shot-gun the other night when that Brown feller had me sort of pinned. Could have been you, Sam, seeing as your window's facing that way. Whoever it was I'd like to — '

'Susan did it,' interjected Sam. 'Said I wasn't to let on to you, but shucks, I guess you ought to know who's on your side.'

Bellamy looked startled. 'Susan! Well, I never guessed — '

Susan flushed. 'I didn't want it to get

around that I was blastin' off with a shot-gun. Folks might think it peculiar. It wouldn't have happened if Father hadn't been restless with pain. He woke me up and I got to looking out of the window and, in the moonlight, I saw Brown prowling about in front of the hotel. A minute later I heard a horse coming and saw Brown flatten against the side of the building. Then you appeared, so I — I got the gun down.'

'So you got the gun down,' Bellamy said softly.

Sam burst in with a chuckle. 'Near lifted me clean outa bed when she let fly with the first barrel. I bawls out, 'what's that' and she calls back, 'a snake'. Then wham goes the other barrel.'

Bellamy said very quietly: 'Thanks, Susan. Thanks and goodnight to you. You too, Sam,' he added almost as an after-thought.

As he pulled the door shut behind him he heard the sound of a bar being dropped in its sockets then turned his attention to the sound of a violent altercation taking place further up the street. When he got to the scene he found four men trading punches. He was minded to let them carry on until they were tired, when one of them drew back and grabbed drunkenly for his gun. Bellamy took three quick strides and drove his fist to the point of the man's jaw. The man went down and did not move.

One of the others yelled out: 'Hey, look what the doggone marshal's done to Oregon.'

The next moment Bellamy was being assaulted from three angles. He stopped the first man's rush with a savage right to his stomach but one of the remaining two lifted a boot and kicked at his shins. Hopping with pain Bellamy saw that the fourth man was clawing at his gun. He launched himself forward, head down, and butted the gun clawer under the chin. He, also, went down without trying to get up. Bellamy whirled about and slung a punch at the man nearest him, knocking him spinning to the ground.

The last man of all hesitated.

'Got some sense left, have you?' Bellamy growled. 'Well, toss that gun of yours in the dirt an' get the guns off the other three.'

The man did as he was told. Bellamy followed it up with another order. 'Now go get the horses of the four of you. Remember to come back, else I'll come looking for you.'

A few seconds later the man returned leading four horses. Bellamy helped him to get his three companions sufficiently conscious to climb up to, and remain in, the saddle then he said:

'Now get out of town, you can collect your guns at my office next time you ride this way.'

As the four moved away Bellamy followed them and stopped outside the saloon. If he could manage the drunks a few at a time as they came out of the saloon, he might be able to avoid shooting, with the possible deaths of men, decent enough in their sober sense. What he could not decide in his own mind was Kerney's angle in feeding the men all this free liquor. The talk Kerney had given him about standing the boys a treat out of generosity was just so much eyewash.

Bellamy had an uneasy feeling that a good deal of deep villainy lay behind Kerney's open-handed gesture. He let half an hour crawl by, during which nothing happened except that the uproar from the saloon became even greater. Then half-a-dozen men came stamping out through the batwings. Bellamy stepped quickly back into deep shadow, prepared, if necessary to break up anything they might start, but to his surprise the six men mounted quietly and rode off.

Something was wrong, very definitely wrong about their behaviour. By Bellamy's accounting, most if not all, should have been at least rolling drunk, but these men acted as if they had not tasted liquor in twenty-four hours.

He moved to the centre of the street and watched their leisurely progress, made out with some difficulty in the darkness that they had reached the end of the street and watched for their emergence from the shadow where the trail rose a little as it left the town. In a few minutes they should be silhouetted against the moonlight but minutes passed and there was no sign of the men.

On a sudden impulse Bellamy crossed to the stables and quickly saddled up. He led his mount out just in time to see a bunch of struggling, shouting men in and around the batwings. A gun roared and a man yelled, then suddenly, bunches of shouting, swearing men erupted into the street. More shots sounded, this time from inside the saloon, and as Bellamy came forward, the lights of the place went out almost as one. With the sudden blotting out of the light that had flooded from doors and windows it was impossible to make out what was going on. Then, from up the street came the thud of galloping horses. Bellamy turned his own mount from the bedlam in front of him and spurred towards the sound of the hoofs.

In another minute he was among the galloping horses, and six-guns were spewing flames and lead in every direction.

With a curse Bellamy drove at the nearest rider, grappled with a half-seen adversary and tore him from his saddle. He checked and swung his mount and pounded after the riders who had torn past him. Then, guns in front of him started to add to the clamour of noise, the guns of the half-drunk, and now madly inflamed range-hands. They shot it out with the galloping horsemen for a few seconds then broke and ran on swaying feet for cover. The horsemen whirled about and Bellamy added the thunder of his own guns. A riderless horse cannoned into his mount, throwing himself and the roan to the ground. For only a moment he lay half stunned, then, the urgency of the business strong upon him, rocketed to his feet.

The horsemen had whirled about again and were pounding down the street a third time. Bellamy's gun lifted one from the saddle, then they were past him and lost in the darkness again. He found his own mount stamping about and squealing, threw himself into the saddle and spurred after the horsemen. He reached the fork at the end of the street and hauled on his reins strongly. The roan slid to a halt. Baffled by the forked trail he swung the horse round again. From up near the saloon came the banging and roaring of the guns. Guns held in the hands of men too drunk to know what they were shooting at.

Bellamy sawed his reins indecisively. The gang on horseback could have ridden off, content with the upset they had caused but he did not think so. There was something more behind the move than just shooting up the town. He had half decided to wait where he was when a deafening roar shook the air around him accompanied by flashes of red and orange flame. Bellamy pushed his mount up the street into a dense cloud of smoke and dust and sensed, rather than saw, men running past him in a direction away from the town. Then, as the sound of pounding hoofs came to his ears, gave a grunt of disgust. This night he had been outwitted more than once. The men he had sensed running past him in the darkness were the same men who had galloped through the town. They must have jumped from their mounts, run back into town, caused the explosion then doubled back to their mounts again.

The dust cloud was settling now, settling enough for him to see a group of men coming towards him. They stopped opposite the store, or what had been the store, for even in the darkness it was possible to see the gaping holes in the structure.

Bellamy slid from the saddle and joined the crowd of men, most of whom still held guns in their hands. He rapped out his words:

'You men holster those guns. There won't be anymore shooting tonight. Any of you that has legs that'll carry you go get lanterns.'

A few men shuffled off in the darkness and came back carrying hurricane lamps.

Bellamy took one and went closer to the shattered building. Not only was it a complete ruin but the shack on either side of the place had been pitched to a crazy angle. One of the shacks was empty and near derelict. The other was the home of Mrs Corran. Bellamy knocked on the crazily hanging door. To his relief a voice sounded from inside.

'I'm all right, just can't open the door an' everything is kinda knocked sideways.'

Bellamy said softly: 'Just stand away from the door, Mrs Corran, I'll get some of the boys help me open it.'

Mrs Corran's voice came in a shrill scream. 'Don't you dare touch that

154

door, young feller. Not 'til I find where my clothes are.'

One of the men laughed; a high pitched laugh of relief.

They waited a few minutes, during which Mrs Corran kept up an almost continuous shrill of commands for them to keep out, then, when the old woman gave her permission, levered open the twisted door. Susan Moss appeared out of the darkness and took Mrs Corran to her own shack.

More lanterns and men appeared, then horses and ropes were brought and the shambles of woodwork, indescribably mixed with goods of all kinds, was dragged and levered into the open street.

It was near to dawn when the men found what they were looking for.

Banks, scarcely marked, was dead.

Bellamy wiped the grime from his hands on some wool material, gave a hitch to his gunbelts and walked purposely toward the saloon. He was through with waiting for definite proof.

Kerney was the man behind all this and the sooner Kerney had a bullet through him the better.

To Bellamy's surprise the saloon's outer door was wide open. He stepped carefully through the batwings, alert for a possible trap. Grey dawn light came through chinks in the window shutters and more widely over the tops of the batwings, showing tables flung out of their places and chairs overturned. Bellamy halted just inside the door. Once again, things did not add up. The door he had just walked through had not been burst open and Kerney had managed to get the shutters on the windows. Surely, he would first bar the door? Still alert for anything that might happen Bellamy moved slowly round the walls of the place, his eyes searching through the gloom and shadow.

He had made almost a complete circuit and was close to one end of the bar when he made out the body of a man on the floor. From the bulk of the man it was Kerney. Bellamy moved closer and after a moment, dropped to his knees. It was Kerney all right and he seemed unconscious. Bellamy straightened up and unbarred the nearest shutter, letting a shaft of grey light fall on Kerney's outstretched bulk. A ragged wound across a swelling lump on Kerney's temple showed why the big man lay inert. Bellamy's glance was cold. He had come to kill this man — to let him go through the formality of grabbing at his gun before putting a slug through him. Now Kerney was in no state to make that grab. Bellamy half turned to leave the man where he was, then it occurred to him that Kerney would have to make some explanation if he roused him from his unconscious state. Some lying explanation probably, but one from which he might glean some truth, for whoever had knocked Kerney out had been someone whom the saloon owner trusted. How else account for the unbarred door?

Bellamy went behind the bar for a jug of cold water and in the poor light nearly stumbled down an opened trap door. About to throw the trap shut again he saw that the heavy lock on it had been wrenched. Bellamy forgot the water he had come for and descended the steep ladder to the cellar. He struck matches until he found a lamp then spent some time looking round the place.

There was not a great deal of liquor stock left and the natural rock wall of the place showed dull and damp in the light of the lamp. Nevertheless, Bellamy came out of the place with a gleam of satisfaction in his eyes.

Kerney could rouse himself from his unconscious slumber. More, he could live for a while yet.

In the street again Bellamy remembered the messenger from Durango and quickly crossed to the office. The man had gone and so had his mount from the lean-to at the back of the office.

Bellamy heaved a sigh of relief. For a moment he had feared that the man had found last night's excitement too tempting and had joined in the general battle.

He came out of the office, his mind back on Kerney. Who had given him that crack on the head? Someone he trusted enough to open the door to, apparently. Smith or Lawson most likely. He had seen the pair amongst the riders shooting up the town. They would realize that too and would know better than to show their faces in Red Rock again. It would be typical of them too, to try to rob Kerney before quitting the place for good.

8

After leaving the office Bellamy went to his room and cleaned himself up. It was still very early when he crossed to Seth Cavan's place for his breakfast.

Seth served him without his usual flow of chatter then said suddenly:

'Lots of folks is pulling out of Red Rock. Guess I'd pull out myself if I had me a wagon. Ain't no use without a wagon, though.'

Bellamy looked up. 'How many's pulling out?'

''Bout half the town, I guess. Some of 'em's fixin' to share a wagon an' team between them, seein' there ain't nearly enough wagons to go round.'

Bellamy sat for a moment in shocked silence. It was true he had forecast to Sam Moss and his daughter the slow death of the town, but such a sudden exodus had never entered his mind.

Again he thought of killing Kerney, but realized he had left it too late. It would take more explanation of Kerney's intentions than it was safe to give, to stop folk leaving town. And if he told everything that he guessed at, the town would explode with violence.

Another surprise awaited Bellamy when he came out of Cavan's place. Two wagons were drawn up outside the saloon and Kerney, a bandage round his head, was superintending the loading of them. Bellamy crossed to speak to him but Kerney got his word in first.

'I'm quitting, Bellamy, pulling out while I've got a sound hide. Last night was plenty for me.'

The words shook Bellamy. Had he been wrong in figuring Kerney as the brain behind all the recent criminal activity? More to get time in which to think than for any other reason, he said:

'What happened to your head, slug graze it?'

Kerney's answer was prompt. 'Someone bounced me — with the butt of a six-gun, I guess. Didn't see who it was, it was too dark. Whoever it was cleaned the till right out.'

'How come? Some jasper break in?'

Kerney shook his head. 'No. Whoever it was, was in all the time. When the shooting started 'most everyone piled out into the street. Me an' Joe got the shutters up, pronto then Joe took it on the run and I barred the door. Reckoned I was alone.' He fingered the lump underneath the bandage. 'I wasn't though.'

Bellamy thought for a moment. Two things indicated that Kerney was lying. One, the fact that he himself found him unconscious just after dawn when, according to Kerney he had been knocked cold sometime bordering on midnight. Bellamy's knowledge on that subject told him that, with such a bump Kerney was not likely to be out for nearly five hours. The other fact was what Bellamy had seen in Kerney's cellar. It would be interesting to see how he left that cellar.

He said: 'Guess my job as marshal'll fold up now. 'Least, there won't be anyone to look to for wages, not with you and Banks gone.'

Kerney nodded. 'A feller like you won't have to travel far to pick up a job.'

'Sure, that's so.'

Bellamy walked away. Farther down the street he found several wagons loading up with a few pitiful possessions. Everyone said they were making for Durango first, and most had borrowed horses from Kerney, the stage horses Kerney had brought from Holden. Bellamy found himself worrying about the people that were remaining in the town, then discovered he was knocking on the door of the Mosses's shack.

Susan opened the door to him and the serious set of her face changed to a smile when she saw who it was. Bellamy entered and came straight to the point.

'Sam, you and Susan have to quit this town. Stay out maybe a week, maybe more. Most other folk are pulling out today.'

Susan's mouth set in a firm line. 'The others, Jeff, those that aren't leaving today — have you asked why they are staying?'

Bellamy shook his head. 'No, I ain't asked that, Susan.'

'It's because they haven't got horses nor the money to hire them, and that's why we're staying.'

'But, gosh dern it, Sue. I'll get horses for you. Steal 'em if I have to.'

'Not for us you won't. We pay our way and take nothing from anyone.'

Bellamy scratched his head. 'Sorry, folks. Guess I ain't used to dealing with decent people. But lookit, here. 'Cording to the way I think, Kerney's going to do all he can to clear this town of people. I'll be surprised if there ain't some more shennanigans tonight. Wouldn't like either of you to get hurt. How if you move to the marshal's office? It's a strong place and — '

'We'll stay right where we are like other folks'll have to. They can't all crowd into the marshal's office.'

Bellamy masked the anger rising within him. 'OK, I'm doing my best.' He picked up his hat and left.

Before noon a long string of creaking wagons rolled out of town, the teams guided by men who were silent. In some cases women, equally silent, sat by the side of the men. Even the few children that rode with them made little noise. In the same dead silence those few that remained watched the exodus.

Bellamy watched the little procession from the front of the marshal's office. He felt restless and uneasy — had a feeling that he too should be riding out, pulling clear of this decaying town which, if he guessed rightly, was already doomed.

In the silence that followed he crossed the street and entered the saloon. Kerney had not even bothered to close the doors after him and appeared to have left everything more or less scattered and overturned. The only thing that had altered since Bellamy's earlier visit was that streaks

165

of bright sunlight came through the doorway and the cracks in the window shutters. His feet echoing in the empty building, Bellamy went behind the bar. The trap to the cellar had been closed but no attempt had been made to secure it. He raised the flap and looked down. Beer and spirit barrels had been tumbled into the place until they jambed the entrance. Bellamy smiled thinly. The device was as good as any other to stop prowlers from entering the cellar. No one would bother to try and haul out empty barrels when full ones were to hand.

He shut the trap-door and walked out of the saloon. Mrs Corran had moved into an empty shack close to her own. A few men and women were busy salvaging food and goods from the ruins of the store. Bellamy wandered down the rest of the empty street, a man without a purpose. He stood a long time gazing at the wreckage of the stage buildings. He would very much like to have cleared that wreckage and seen what was underneath, but the chore was impossible without a team of horses and gangs of men. Impossible, at any rate, in the time he figured was left to him.

It was evening before any shred of an idea came to him. Even then it was not much of an idea, but it suddenly occurred to him as peculiar that Kerney, whose two wagons had been loaded well before any of the others, had been the last to leave town.

Bellamy spent some time in thought. The wagons would undoubtedly pause for rest and water for the teams at the halt Zeke had run. Probably they would not stay more than an hour before pushing on again. Kerney, with Joe Sangers driving his second wagon, had left town almost two hours behind the main party.

Bellamy went quickly to the stables, saddled his mount, the only one remaining in the place, and set a fast pace to what he now thought of as Dolly's place.

The first stars were showing in the sky when he came in sight of the buildings. He drew rein and slid from the saddle then led the horse away from the trail. There was no cover to hide his approach but he reasoned that, if he kept well away from the trail there was a fair chance of approaching unobserved.

A hundred yards from the place he left his mount with the reins trailing and went forward by himself. Chinks of light showed from behind shuttered windows as he drew nearer. He made for the window he knew to be the living room. Within a yard of the place a burst of laughter came to his ears. He had no difficulty in identifying the laugh as Dolly's. Coming close to the shutter he listened intently. Dolly's voice, bubbling with laughter, intermingled with a deep, hoarse voice. The words were not intelligible to him but he was certain the deep voice belonged to Kerney. He wondered about Sangers. Was he in there also? Leaving the shuttered window Bellamy moved soft-footed round to the stables. Someone had provided a stout new lock to the doors. His intention to count the horses defeated, he moved back to the window. The pair inside were still laughing and talking. Bellamy eased quietly away from the place. There seemed little reason for staying any longer. Kerney was in the place but whether he was just staying the night or not was impossible to guess.

Halfway back to his mount a sound of distant drumming came to his ears. He hurried over the remaining stretch of ground and grabbed at his mount's reins. The distant drumming resolved itself into the hoof beats of four horses coming from the direction of Durango.

Bellamy mounted, swung his mount further away from the trail and came in a wide circle that brought him directly behind the stables of Dolly's place. In a few more minutes the four horses and their riders came into view and stopped at the door of the shack. The door opened, spilling a wide streak of yellow lamplight into darkness. Kerney's bulk filled the doorway.

One of the riders said: 'OK, boss, we're here.'

Kerney grunted. 'I can see that. Well, you know what to do. Clean the whole place up — that blasted marshal included if you can get him. Now, don't try shooting it out with him, remember he's more than good with guns. Fire and gun powder are what you want to use.'

Bellamy gave a cluck of satisfaction. Kerney had exposed himself at last. For a moment Bellamy thought of charging in and using his guns but reflection told him that the clatter of his mount's hoofs would cause the four riders to scatter and Kerney to dive inside and barricade the place. He might easily lose all four in the darkness and with them scattered about could not easily lay seige to Kerney. There was Dolly too. How deep was she in with Kerney? The four were now swinging away from the shack and the wide swathe of light coming from the doorway was suddenly cut off as the door slammed shut.

Bellamy let the men ride clear then walked his own mount away from the stables and the trail before letting the roan have its head across the rough ground. His aim was to draw ahead of the four riders and come to the trail again in front of them. Only by reaching town before them and confronting them in the very street of the place could he be assured of destroying all four, and he wanted no straggler able to make his way to Kerney. Kerney, he promised himself, was due for a surprise visit, with himself as his last visitor on earth.

The roan was blowing heavily when he swung it back again to the trail and he would have had doubts of a lesser animal reaching the town without collapsing. He stopped for a few seconds and sat listening intently. A faint drumming told him he had overtaken the four riders. He shook up his mount again and, in spite of its labouring wind, it settled down into a long, raking stride. Somewhere between two and three in the morning he led the roan into its stable, hastily pulled off the saddle and threw a blanket over the lathered animal. There was not time to do more as the four could only be minutes behind him at the most.

Coming into the street the sound of hoofs was clear on the silence of the night. Bellamy decided to meet the oncoming riders right where the first shacks began the street. There would be no fancy work, no calling on them to draw. Just shots the moment they were in range.

He positioned himself against the end of the very last shack, a place he knew to be empty. In three minutes the riders were in sight. He waited until they covered another few hundred yards then both his guns came out and into action. He must have been seen by the riders at the moment he drew, for suddenly the horses swerved wildly.

With his first shots Bellamy lifted one man from his saddle, another yelled with pain and swung his mount away at a gallop. The other two, after a few half-hearted shots that went wild, hauled their mounts almost on their haunches before spurring madly from the scene.

Bellamy holstered his guns and walked forward to glance at the man who lay dead. He was a stranger, and Bellamy wondered how many more gunslingers Kerney had hired from outside.

He caught the horse and looked it over as best he could in the moonlight. It did not seem to be much of a mount but it would probably serve to carry him to Kerney which the roan would not do, having already done the double journey. He threw himself into the saddle and let the horse make its own pace.

It would reach Dolly's place not much after daylight.

Kerney, after the four riders had left for Red Rock, seemed to be an entirely different character. He became more expansive, genial and talkative. He also drank carelessly. A thing he had never done before. He fondled and pawed Dolly on every occasion that she came anywhere near him. Dolly, at first not averse to this, grew a little more practical as the time went on. She wanted to know more precisely just what scheme Kerney had, wanted to know just where, and how, the fabulous wealth that he kept promising would be theirs was to come from. But Kerney, in spite of becoming a little drunk would not let her know the final details.

Dolly took Kerney's amorousness in her stride. Used to handling all types of men she had calculated just exactly how much pressure to put on Kerney to make him say what she wanted to hear. She gave a vast yawn and stretched her hands above her head.

'Gosh, I'm tired. Guess I'll hit the hay. See you in the morning.'

Kerney grabbed her to him. 'In the morning, hell!'

Dolly wriggled free. 'Oh, I'm tired, 'sides, you only talk a lot of nonsense about how rich we'll be, an' a girl can't keep an interest in just rumours.'

Kerney shook his head. 'They're not rumours, Dolly. They're solid fact. Solid as gold.'

Dolly smiled archly, patting him on the cheek: 'OK, big boy, but I'm still tired an' I guess those solid facts'll keep 'til morning. Goodnight.'

She made a quick move towards her own room. Kerney followed, grabbing hold of her again. His voice, thick with passion and liquor, rumbled in her ear.

Dolly thought rapidly. Kerney's mutterings had given her a vision of the sort of wealth that had never even entered her head. Even so, the prospect was not entirely inviting. Life with this big slug pawing and slobbering over her could be just another kind of hell, even with all the dough to spend. When Kerney had first proposed that she join him in a scheme which, he claimed, would eventually make the town his own and hers also, she had accepted mainly with a view of getting rid of Zeke and, at the same time, gathering together enough money to make herself independent. She had visioned herself queening over some big saloon, Kerney's partner up to a point, but not up to the point of selling herself to him. Now, she saw several more enticing prospects before her than being Kerney's woman.

But a man was needed if she was to succeed, and there was only one man who stood tall enough for this deal.

'Let's have some more drink, let's have one real humdinger of a night. Gosh, news like that'd put any gal right on her toes.'

She crossed to the cupboard where she kept the liquor, flung the door wide and slammed it shut again.

'Hell, we used up the last bottle.'

Kerney grinned widely. 'Plenty on that second wagon of mine. I'll go and — '

Dolly snatched up a hurricane lamp. 'Leave it to me. I know that crazy barn door better'n you do.'

176

She put a match to the lamp and whirled through the door. Kerney chuckled to himself. Nothing like real dough for bringing a woman to heel, he thought.

Five minutes later he let out a startled curse as the drumming of a horse's hoofs came to his ears. Quickly, he blew at the light and then moved to the doorway, gun in hand. It was some seconds before it dawned on him that the beating hoofs were drawing away from him, not coming closer. Even then it took more time for him to realize it might be Dolly who was riding away.

He lumbered over to the barn, found it still locked then, with a curse, turned to the stable alongside it. The door of that was locked also. Swearing freely he fired shots into the lock until it gave then wrenched open the door. Startled horses squealed and lashed out in fear as he entered. He struck a match to find the lamp that should be hanging in the place. He saw it by the first flicker of the flame — overturned and stamped nearly flat. In almost a panic now he made as much speed as his great bulk allowed back to the shack. Wrenching the hanging lamp from its fastening on the rafters Kerney lumbered back to the stable, seized on a saddle and bridle and spent a frantic ten minutes getting the gear on a frightened, stamping horse.

He came out of the stable on the run and had difficulty getting into the saddle. Once mounted he treated his horse without mercy, jerking at the reins and using the heel of his boots as spurs. The horse, ears flattened and teeth bared, did its best and held a mad gallop for the best part of a mile but it was a lightly built animal and no match for Kerney's great weight plus the way he was riding it. In spite of the big man's yelled curses and savage heeling at its flanks the animal under him began to slow up. But not until his mount was labouring for breath did Kerney realize the folly of his methods. Then it was he started to think again. What had been Dolly's aim in cutting loose and flying to town unless it was that she had made some previous arrangement? Some arrangement that depended on her finding out what his ultimate end was. If so, it could only be with Bellamy, and Bellamy, by now, ought to have his hands full. In fact, there was a possibility that Bellamy was dead. The man's infernal good luck could not last for ever.

Kerney decided to let his mount take an easier pace and to approach Red Rock with caution. He also decided that Dolly had reached the end of her run. A pity, because he fancied Dolly, but there were other women.

Dolly's thoughts as she pounded along the trail centred on Bellamy. She figured she was an hour and thirty minutes behind the gang that had gone to clean up Red Rock and, if possible, to get him. Surely a man of his fighting powers would be able to hold off four gunslingers for that long? She had a vague plan which she hoped to be able to put into effect when she got into Red

Rock. She hoped to make contact with the gang and to persuade them into believing that Kerney had sent her with orders to hold off Bellamy. It depended on Bellamy being alive, of course, and on herself being able to talk fast enough, for she realized that Kerney would not be far behind her.

She was some six miles from the town and coming to the long, downhill slope of the trail when she saw a rider coming towards her. Too late to avoid detection she reined in her mount and waited.

Bellamy's surprise on seeing her was as great as her own. Bellamy acted quickly, one of his powerful hands fastening on her wrist.

'Kerney — where is he?'

She did not try to jerk free. 'Right behind me somewhere. Let's get off the trail — quick.'

'Why?' The single word snapped out.

'Because I've got something important to tell you, and Kerney'll kill me if he catches up with me.'

Bellamy thought rapidly. He wanted everything he could get against Kerney before killing him. Dolly would be better out of the way when the lead began to fly.

'Over here,' he said curtly. 'There's a shoulder of rock'll give us cover.'

Dolly spurred after him. As soon as they were behind the rock Bellamy slid from the saddle and put his ear to the ground.

'He's not caught up with you yet,' he announced as he straightened up.

'I made it as bad for him as I could,' Dolly said. 'He sent four men to — '

'I know. Forget about them. What's this important thing you have to tell me?'

'I found out what Kerney's scheme is.'

'Know about that myself. What made you suddenly change sides?'

'Change sides? How — '

'You were at the door when Kerney sent that gang to clean up on me and the town. Remember his words about using fire and gunpowder?'

'Well, I had to find out for certain just what Kerney was up to.'

'And now you've found out?'

Dolly hesitated for a moment, her eyes striving to make out, in the dim starlight, something of Bellamy's face. Failing, she said:

'I thought if I shared the information with you, you'd — oh, hell, you know dern well what I'm trying to say.'

Bellamy touched her arm. 'No, don't say it, Dolly. It wouldn't have been that way, in any case, and as I found out about Kerney before you told me — well, there's nothing to your information. Sorry, you seem to have lost out every way. Kerney'll be dead the minute he rides in gun range. You'd better stay here a while.'

He climbed to the saddle and started his mount walking toward the trail.

Dolly watched his back, her lips curving in a savage snarl.

'Cut me out would you, you big louse?'

Her hand dived into a pocket in her skirt and came out again with a short barrelled revolver. She fired two shots in rapid succession, aiming for the middle of Bellamy's back.

Bellamy reeled in his saddle, one hand clawed towards a gun then he pitched sideways to the ground.

Dolly scrambled on to her own mount and spurred away from the spot.

9

Bellamy came to his senses slowly. It was some minutes before he could lift himself off the ground. Then he stood weaving about like a drunken man. Conscious first of a hot, stabbing pain where his belt rubbed at his back he explored the place with his fingers, felt a groove in the top of his belt and drew his hand away wet and sticky with blood. More blood was pouring down the left side of his shoulder from a crease just below his ear. Hazily, he realized that his wide, thick belt had taken some of the force from the slug that had penetrated just below his ribs. The wound on his neck did not matter so much except that it was bleeding freely.

He made a pad of his bandanna and handkerchief and bound it over the neck wound as best as he could. The other wound, the one in his back, would need other hands to attend to it.

He saw the dim, outlined bulk of the horse he had been riding, standing nearby and staggered over to it. With both hands on the saddle he tried to hoist himself on to the animal and had half succeeded when a great weakness came over him and he slipped to his knees. From somewhere distant a gun boomed twice while he tried to raise himself to his feet again. He managed it only by hanging on to the stirrup leather and then had to lean against the saddle while he panted for breath. In a muddled fashion he wondered who had been doing the shooting, then set his teeth for another effort to climb to the saddle. He got half way on to the animal's back when it started to move. Cursing weakly he pulled it to a standstill and clawed his foot round for a stirrup. Finding it at last he heaved his other leg astride the beast and, half slumped across its neck, let it make its own way.

In the first grey of the dawn the horse

wandered into the town and stood disconsolately outside the stable, waiting for the immobile burden on its back to climb down and open the door.

Sam Moss, who like most of the others in Red Rock, had been roused by the firing of Bellamy's guns earlier and had afterwards not dared to go to sleep, came out of his shack at first light and found Bellamy slumped forward over the animal's neck. He led the horse to his own door and, with the help of Susan, somehow hauled Bellamy from the saddle and got him on to a bed. Serious though the wound in Bellamy's back appeared at first sight, it proved not so bad as Sam feared. When cleaned it showed that a small calibre slug had been half deflected by Bellemy's belt and then ripped upwards to lodge against a rib. Sam and Susan between them did nearly as much for Bellamy as a doctor could have done.

In the mid-afternoon Bellamy opened his eyes, stared vacantly at the ceiling for a few moments then turned his head.

His eyes lighted first on Susan then on Sam.

Bellamy grinned. ' 'Lo, folks, how'd I get here?'

He made an effort to lift himself upright.

Susan moved quickly forward. 'You're not to move. You're to lie still. I'll get you some soup.'

She hurried into the other room. Bellamy's eyes sought Sam's. 'How come, Sam?'

'Found you half on, an' half off, some old plug of a hoss right outside the stable.'

Susan came in with the soup. 'You're to quit talking, Jeff, and drink this.'

With Sam's help she raised him a little in the bed. Bellamy spooned the soup hungrily then handed her the empty bowl.

'Thanks, Sue. You sure make good soup. Now I've got to talk a space. Does anyone else know I'm here? 'Cause if so, someone'll likely come gunning for me.'

Sam shook his head. 'I shouldn't think so. It was barely light when Sue an' me hauled you in, an' there weren't no one about.'

Susan added. 'I've been out since and talked to one or two folks. There's plenty of talk about there being one dead man found just at the end of the street and Dolly Smethers being found about a mile up the trail, but no mention of you being seen. In fact, the general idea seems to be that you've lit out.'

'They'll figure it different if anyone goes in the stable. My horse is there an' I ain't seen to him properly. What's this about Dolly Smethers?'

Susan gave him a shrewd look. 'Thought you might know about that. That slug we took out of your back about matches up with the gun Dolly had in her pocket. The gun had been fired twice.'

'Sure, I know it was Dolly that plugged me all right,' Bellamy said irritably. 'What I want to know is, what's Dolly doing now?'

'Dolly ain't doin' anythin',' Sam grunted. 'Dolly stopped two forty-five slugs at close range.'

Bellamy jerked upright. 'Hell, Dolly was bad all right, but not bad enough for that.'

'She shot you in the back,' Susan reminded him.

'Yeah, that's so. Guess she was kind of sore when she tried to sell me a gold mine that I already knew about.'

'A gold mine!' Sam interjected.

'That's right, that's what Kerney figures. Slap underneath where Holden had his freight office. 'Cording to what Dolly spilled just before she plugged me, Kerney's got hold of some old prospector's chart that says it's so. I made a guess at something of the sort just before Kerney cleared out. Got down in that liquor cellar of his and saw someone had been picking at the rock face — taking samples, I guess. After that, I did a bit of figuring myself. That rock face in Kerney's cellar runs slap along the edge of the town and outcrops where Holden had his outfit.'

Sam's eyes moved away from Bellamy's face. 'I reckon you ought to be restin', Jeff. It ain't right for me to keep you yammerin'. I heard something like that years back. Guess it was the same rumour that caused this town to be built — '

'Sam, you're hidin' something,' Bellamy said quietly. 'Something I guess I ought to know.'

Sam moved uncomfortably. 'Well, it's like this, Jeff. That rock in Kerney's cellar mebbe has colour, but — Well there ain't enough gold for one good drunk. I know because — ' He stopped, a confused look on his face. 'You get some rest, Jeff — '

Bellamy jerked upright and as he did so a spasm of pain crossed his face. He appeared about to say something and then fell back on the pillow.

Susan flew to his side. 'Father — ' she shrilled. 'I knew this would happen. Get fresh rags for bandages. Gosh almighty, look at that blood.'

Working on redressing the wound she and Sam stopped the new flow of blood, and presently Bellamy passed from a half conscious state into sleep. It was two whole days before he opened his eyes for long enough to recognize anything. When he did, Susan was at his side.

'Move or talk, and so help me I'll leave you to die,' she told him.

Three days later Bellamy got his feet to the floor. Immediately he demanded to know all that had happened.

Sam Moss handed him a letter. 'A guy brought this for you. I just happened on him when he was coming out of the hotel after finding no one there. We had a kind of a long talk together. Sort of finding out whose side each other was on, then I brought the guy in here an' showed him how you were. Hope I did right.'

Bellamy slit the envelope. 'You did right, an' thanks for being so careful.'

He read the letter from Lincoln Jones. It told him that Kerney had paid Holden with a cheque and that the

191

cheque had not yet found its way into any bank. Lin also said that the sheriff was taking an unsual amount of interest in the killing of Holden.

'How about Kerney? Seen anything of him?' Bellamy asked when he had read the letter.

'Nary a sign,' Sam answered. 'Seth Cavan an' three other men pulled out yesterday. Reckons they'll make Durango on foot in five or six days. There's some others that'll never be able to walk that far.'

'They won't have to,' Bellamy snapped reaching for his shirt. 'The moment Kerney shows his face in town I'll put a bullet through him. We can settle who owns the property later.'

Susan came into the room just as Bellamy had finished dressing and was buckling on his gunbelt. Her eyes widened in surprise.

'Jeff Bellamy, just what are you doing? It might be all right for you to get up for a spell but what's the idea of the gunbelt?'

Bellamy grinned at her. 'Might need the gun. 'Sides, I don't feel dressed without it. What's doing in town?'

'Three wagons coming down the street from Durango way, and hardly any food left in the place. I've been foraging in the ruins of the store like everyone else has to. Got a few cans but I guess that's about the last.'

'Wagons!' Bellamy said sharply. 'Wagons are just what this town needs.'

He made for the door. Susan gave a cry of alarm.

'You're not fit to go out — '

But Bellamy was already out and looking at three two-horse wagons rumbling slowly towards him. The wagons were piled high with goods, and six men, besides the drivers, clung to various parts of the loads. Bellamy planted himself in the middle of the street and raised his hand. The wagons rolled to a halt.

'What is it, Mister?' the leading driver called.

Bellamy appraised the man before

answering. Obviously, he was neither a gunslinger nor a range man.

'I'm marshal of this town. What goes on, an' where are you heading?'

The driver spat tobacco juice. 'Understood this was a ghost town. No one told me 'bout there bein' a marshal. We got a diggin' chore on. This place is supposed to be a strike. I got papers that say me an' the boys should get diggin'.' His eyes wandered to Bellamy's guns. 'Ain't aimin' to argue with those guns of yours though.'

Bellamy nodded. 'Drive up to the fork an' unload your wagons there. Start in digging if that's what you're paid to do, but this town needs the loan of your wagons and teams.'

'Say, now, Marshal!'

'I thought you didn't want an argument? Get going, we want two of those wagons and a driver for each.'

The wagons rolled to the end of the street and the men began to unload. Bellamy went back into Sam Moss's shack and sat down. He felt weak and shaky but wanted desperately to think clearly and there seemed so much to think about. The wagons he had commandeered he intended sending to Durango for necessary supplies but unless he himself went with them how could he be sure of their safe arrival, much less their return? Would he be able to stand up to the double journey and still remain a useful man in case of trouble? If only he knew for certain where Kerney was he could ride out and take care of him. Or was it necessary to kill Kerney now? What would Kerney's reactions be when he discovered that the gold he sought was non-existent? Bellamy's spinning head seemed not to be able to cope with the questions.

Susan looked at him. 'I told you, you weren't fit to go out.'

Kerney too, had difficulties, also some fears. Since the night he had shot Dolly he had found several things to worry about. Dolly had protested her innocence loudly when he had caught up with her just on the edge of the town, and had sworn vehemently that she had killed Bellamy and left his body some five or six miles back from town and away from the edge of the trail. She had talked so convincingly about the killing that he had believed that part of the story, but not the rest. So he had shot her in the middle of her protestations.

Only after he had made a trip to Durango and engaged a team of hard rock miners to work for him in Red Rock had it occurred to him that he ought to verify Dolly's statement that she had put two slugs into Bellamy's back. Leaving Dolly's shack which, since he had killed her, he had used as his own, Kerney rode out one dawn seeking the place Dolly had so vividly talked about. Uneasily the eyes of the big man searched the ground which was mostly bald rock and held only thin patches of soil. Seeing no sign of the dead body he looked for, he climbed down from the saddle and prowled around on foot. Eventually he found the hoof prints of two horses, then further on, some scars on the ground where apparently something had been dragged for a short distance.

No reader of trail signs, Kerney climbed back on his saddle, a growing uncertainty gnawing at his mind.

Bellamy might be dead or he might not. Kerney could not figure on anyone else learning of the shooting and coming out to recover Bellamy's body or, alternatively, carry him wounded into town. There could be only himself and Dolly who knew of the shooting and Dolly had died before she could talk to anyone else, he was certain of that. It seemed that Bellamy must be alive — and alive after talking to Dolly.

Kerney's thoughts filled him with rage, a rage in which fear had a good share. Bellamy must know about the gold and that being so would be doubly anxious to kill him.

Kerney came back to the Smethers' shack with a new resolve. Even a man of Bellamy's character was not bullet proof nor, clever as the man seemed, did he have eyes in his back.

Kerney saw to his mount, barred the door and went to sleep until late evening. Rising, he made himself a meal, saddled a fresh horse and, with a Winchester across the saddle bow, made for the town. He rode slowly, keeping clear of the trail, and a mile away from the town climbed down from the saddle. It was long past midnight when, rifle in hand, he came to the end of the street. Skirting round the back of the property he came to his deserted saloon from the side. He waited in the deeper shadows for a long time before venturing to put foot on the veranda and was certain that no one saw him as he entered the building. Fumbling round in the darkness Kerney found himself a chair and sat down. His scheme seemed to him to have the elements of simplicity that promised success. Bellamy, if alive and fit enough to be about was an early riser. Wherever

Bellamy was hived down he would be out with the dawn to see to his horse. The stable door was almost directly opposite the saloon and the Winchester could hardly miss at such close range.

Bellamy's spell of weakness, far from passing away, became worse as he listened to Susan's gentle upbraiding of him with a growing realization that she was right. Whatever the outcome he would have to rest awhile. In any case it was getting late in the day to organise a wagon trip to Durango. The few people left in Red Rock could manage for just one more day. He said wearily:

'Guess I'll lie down for a spell, Sue.'

'I should think you will. All the trouble Father and I have had to get you fixed up and you have to go stamping round the street.'

Sam grinned. 'She was jus' the same with me, Jeff, when I wanted to limber around. Guess you'll have to put up with it for a spell.'

Bellamy did put up with it to the extent of unbuckling his gunbelt, pulling off his boots and lying on the shake-down. But no amount of bullying or cajoling by Susan could persuade him to go back to bed again. He spent the rest of the day sleeping and resting and when nightfall came, insisted on staying where he was.

Around midnight he found himself restless and wakeful and lay for a while staring at the thin rays of the moonlight. Finally, an unbearable thirst made him get up and pad softly across the room for a dipper of water. He drank deeply then stood staring out of the window into the silent street. About to go back to his shake-down he noticed a shadowy figure slip across the space between the two shacks on the opposite side of the street. It took him less than a minute to drag on his boots and snatch up his gunbelt before slipping silently out of doors.

The side of the street on which he was, lay deep in shadow while the other side was coloured with the soft light of the steadily climbing moon. He hesitated for a moment then moved stealthily down the street, pausing at intervals to listen. Opposite the hotel he stood for a while watching for any movement then moved again until the entrance to Kerney's saloon was in line. Again he stood listening and this time there came a faint scraping noise. The sound had undoubtedly come from the opposite side of the street, possibly from the saloon itself. He felt an urgent need to get across to the other side of the street to investigate. He moved back quickly the way he had come then went further until he was well beyond Sam Moss's shack. Reason told him that the figure he had seen move quickly across the space had arrived somewhere near the saloon and was the cause of the small noise he had heard. To reach the opposite side of the street he would have to cross a wide swathe of moonlight with every chance of being seen. He had made the chance as small as possible by coming to this end of the street and now, with a quick glance in either direction, hared across. Slipping to the backs of the premises he threaded a quick way between piles of garbage and empty cans, knowing that here, in the cold light of the moon, attempt at concealment was useless.

At the space between the hotel and the saloon he turned in. Eight or ten feet from the ground the window of the saloon which he himself had unshuttered stared blackly. Bellamy eyed the window longingly then realized the futility of his longing. He could certainly reach the sill of the window with a spring and then scramble up, but the noise he would make would amply advertise his coming if anyone was in the saloon. He put his ear against the clapboard sides of the place and remained listening until his neck was cramped by his attitude, then, straightening up, began to move towards the street. He had made four or five slow strides when the scraping noise came again. This time it was comparatively loud and he identified the cause almost with the same certainty as if he had been watching the movement. Someone in the saloon was sitting on a chair and had moved restlessly, causing the legs of the chair to scrape over the rough boards of the floor.

Bellamy ceased his forward movement. He had to know who was in the saloon and for what reason. Entry by the door would be suicidal if the person in there had murderous intentions. The same went for the only window that was unshuttered. There remained the choice of waiting until daylight and finding some way of forcing the man inside the saloon to come out. Then he remembered. In the hallway of the hotel was a rickety looking stepladder. Would it have been left behind when the owner cleared out? He doubled, soft-footed, round to the front of the hotel and stepped gingerly into the entrance between heaps of unwanted debris. Feeling around, because he dared not make a light, he located the ladder and eased it from the rubbish that had been piled against it. He came to the unshuttered window of the saloon with the same animal-like silence of movement and gently put the ladder in place.

A step at a time he went up until his head was level with the window. Twisting himself to an awkward angle he peered into the shadowed depths of the saloon's interior. He could just make out the darker bulk of shadow formed by a man sitting almost by the door of the place. Bellamy's hand went down for a Colt with which to smash in the glass of the window. He had the weapon out of its holster and poised for a quick blow when, without warning, the ladder collapsed under his weight. As he went down the gun in his hand clattered against the glass without breaking it. He fell heavily and awkwardly with the broken pieces of the ladder tangling his legs, and had difficulty getting himself free before jumping up. In the short interval he heard the sound of feet run across the wooden floor and veranda of the saloon. Then down the narrow opening that faced to the street came the sing and whine of slugs while the space seemed filled with an echoing roar and red and white flashes of light. Although his own Colt was still in his hand he went instantly to ground and refrained from firing and so giving the other man something to aim at.

After a few seconds the shooting ceased and again came the sound of running feet, but this time muffled by soft ground. Bellamy came to his feet and took the short distance to the street in a few long strides. His eyes searched the place for any movement, saw none and concluded that whoever had been in the saloon was now haring out of town. He took a step forward that brought him into the street. Instantly there came a sharp crack, easily identified as a rifle and Bellamy's hat went spinning from his head. He ducked to the cover offered by the corner of a building just as a second slug whined through the space he had occupied. The second of the rifle shots had given him a place to aim at and he came half from cover with both Colts roaring. The rifle spat back once and then ceased. Bellamy ducked back to reload. He did not think his slugs had found the man with the rifle as the range had been almost at six-gun limit but guessed that the particular individual had had enough of his present position and had moved on. The thing was, had he decided to quit or would he try a game of hide and seek? Bellamy felt that at the moment he could do nothing but wait until the other showed his hand. His own side of the street was flooded with moonlight while that of his adversary was still heavy with shadow, although the light was creeping steadily towards it.

An hour of patient watching and listening gained him nothing except that the pale light in the street had crept across the full width of it and now offered no shadowy cover on the other side. He crossed the place on the run, expecting at any moment to hear the crack of the rifle but none came. Working his way cautiously up the backs of the buildings he came to the opening the man had used. Entering, he found three empty shell cases, proof enough that he was in the right place and, allied to the silence that had so long prevailed, an indication that the rifleman had departed.

He made his way back to the shack where Susan, wide awake, spent a good quarter of an hour in scolding him before she put on some coffee to brew.

10

Breakfast was over when Bellamy made known, what seemed to him after further thought, the only practical scheme.

Nothing less than the evacuation of Red Rock.

Both Sam and Susan protested that neither he or Kerney would prevail on them to go and that, in any case, they had not the means. Bellamy explained patiently, although it seemed to him that there was more fear than actual reluctance behind their protestations.

'Look, both of you, Kerney's got a legal hold on the whole town,' Bellamy argued. 'Sooner or later he's going to drive you out. The only thing that can stop that is for someone to kill him first. It's my guess that Kerney knows I will try to do just that at the first opportunity. Maybe it was him prowling round last night, trying to get his slug in first, but Kerney doesn't have to play it that way. There's nothing to stop him from sending in more rock miners an' such to tear this town apart. He'll find out some time or other that he's wasting his time, but by then the damage will be done. No, the only thing to do is to make him think we've all quit. Then when he comes I'll see that he stays — only it'll be in a grave of some sort.'

'But that'll be murder,' Susan protested.

'I'll give him a chance to draw, but it'll be murder all right,' Bellamy said grimly. 'Reckon it's the only way, us being outside of the reach of the law. If we were in Durango it'd be different. But we ain't.'

Discussion and argument went on for a long time, but finally Sam and Susan realized that they could not stay much longer in Red Rock so long as Kerney had his way with the place. Susan's last protest that they had no way of travelling, Sam still not being able to walk far, was countered by Bellamy's suggestion that they should club together with the other folk remaining to pay for the loan of the miners' wagons. It seemed the only way of getting over Susan's pride in taking nothing they could not pay for. He intended, however, that the teamsters who had brought the wagons in should lend them and their services at very reasonable rates.

He left Sam and Susan to contact their few neighbours and spread the idea while he went to talk to the wagon drivers.

He walked with his long, slow stride into the camp close to the site of Holden's one-time freight office. All the men stopped whatever they were doing and viewed him with uneasy eyes.

Bellamy had no quarrel with them but thought a little fear might help. He stood silent, a hand on each gun, his eyes travelling slowly from one to the other.

Finally he said in a slow drawl. 'Howdy, fellers. Sure like to borrow a couple of wagons. Like to make a little trip to Durango. Guess it'd take a coupla days either way. Wouldn't like you fellers to be out on the deal but the folk here are sure short on dough. Short on most other things, I guess.'

A man who looked as if he was bossing the outfit answered: 'We'll loan you the teams, an' bring supplies in from Durango an' welcome, Marshal. Guess we could make it there and back in three days.'

Bellamy nodded. 'I thought you might. Folk have changed their minds about stopping, though. They just want to get to Durango with whatever they can carry. They don't aim to come back.'

'Anythin' you say, Marshal. Us fellers don't sling guns an' we don't want no trouble.'

'Be glad if you hitches up an' draws somewhere near the saloon then. Make it right now, will you?'

He turned and walked away, certain that whoever else tried to fight him it would not be these men.

Sam and Susan told him that they had met with little resistance to the idea of leaving Red Rock. Indeed, most of the others would have left with the first out-going people if they had had some kind of transport. Except for Susan and Sam they were all elderly people and unfit to tramp the distance as some of the others had done.

The two wagons rumbled up and Bellamy and Sam helped with the loading. There was little enough to load when all came to all.

When the wagons were ready to roll Susan came to Bellamy. 'We'll pay these men now. Would you ask them how much it is?'

Bellamy called one of the drivers over. 'The lady wants to know how much it's going to be.'

The teamster shuffled his feet and gave a side glance at Bellamy. 'How would ten bucks suit you, Ma'am?'

Susan counted out ten dollars in silver. 'I think you're being very reasonable.'

The teamster's glance wandered to Bellamy's guns. 'Sure, Ma'am. *Very* reasonable.'

Bellamy crossed to the stable and brought out the roan. Susan looked at him in surprise when he climbed into the saddle.

'You didn't say you were coming, Jeff.'

'Ridin' as far as the Smethers' place,' he told her briefly. 'Maybe further. It all depends.'

He kept with the wagons until the Smethers' place was in sight then went ahead at a tearing gallop. Leaving the saddle he tried the door of the shack and found that it opened. Kerney could be inside and waiting for him but Bellamy did not think so. Shots in the dark and from behind cover were more to the saloon owner's taste. However as a precaution he kicked the door wide and jumped to one side at the same time. When no sound came to him he walked rapidly in and assured himself that the place was really empty. He felt the top of the stove and found that it was cold. He threw kindling into it and had a roaring blaze by the time the teams hauled to a halt. Susan took charge of the stove as soon as she entered the place, setting coffee to brew. Bellamy went over to the stables. Here again the doors were not locked. He almost did not go inside, so sure was he that the place held no horses. However, he had to assure himself that the stables were empty.

He went back to the shack in a thoughtful frame of mind. That Kerney had deserted the place seemed evident. On first thought it seemed that he had ducked out of the way of Bellamy himself, but a man in a panic flight does not stop long enough to arrange the removal of a dozen or so horses, and the horses had been there not many hours ago. Bellamy was certain of that from the warm smell the stables still held.

The disappearance of the change horses made a new difficulty. The teams that were hauling the wagons would have to haul them for the whole of the sixty or so miles to Durango. That meant a night's camping by the trail. No great hardship if they were left alone, but if they were not — Bellamy decided to go all the way with the wagons. The people riding in them were, with the exception of Sam and Susan, either old grey beards or women and children.

After an hour's break the party moved on, Bellamy riding at the side of the foremost wagon which held, along with others, Sam and Susan Moss. Bellamy talked little, and then only about things in general. Sam, he noticed, was becoming very tired and shifted his position constantly to ease the ache of the partly healed wounds.

Bellamy called a halt at a point a little more than half way to Durango. The place he had chosen was on high ground and had a few dusty looking trees growing at the edge of a small water course. The sun was still high but it seemed to him that both the horses and the people in the wagons were weary of the trail. He helped to make cooking fires and see to the horses, then a little later, when a meal had been eaten, strolled with Susan to the edge of the stream. Here, there was some coolness and shade, and for a while neither spoke being content to listen to the gurgle of the waters as they rushed on a downhill course. At last Susan said:

'Good place you picked for a camp, Jeff.'

'Not bad. It's got water, and wood for the fires and a mite of shade. Be a little cooler when the sun goes down, maybe.'

She glanced about her. 'You chose it because it's high, open ground too, didn't you?'

Bellamy did not answer for a while, then he said briefly: 'Guess I was born suspicious.' Then, 'Maybe we'd better get back to the others. There's bound to be chores waitin' to be done.'

216

She gave him a wistful glance. 'Jeff, you're a hard man to get close to. What does a woman have to do to make you say what's in your mind?'

He said roughly: 'Minds like mine ain't fit for a woman to know about. Tell Sam to have his gun handy an' sleep with one eye open.'

As soon as they reached the camp Bellamy left her and moved to the highest point of the ground. There, he sat smoking and watching the sun's rays turn the dusty land to red and gold then to purple as it shot it's final rays. Only then did he move to the edge of the camp and fling a blanket on the ground to roll himself in. He slept almost at once and scarcely stirred until the dawn. Then he came sharply up to a sitting position while his hand reached for a Colt that had never been far from his grasp. He listened for a while then caught the faint sound that had roused him — the distant drumming of horses' hoofs. He came to his feet silently and moved to where Sam Moss was sleeping. Sam was instantly awake at the touch of Bellamy's hand and climbed stiffly to his feet.

'Horses,' Bellamy whispered.

Sam listened for a few seconds. 'Yeah, I hear them.'

Bellamy motioned Sam to follow him and the pair cat-footed away from the sleeping camp for some hundreds of yards to take up a position to one side of the trail. Here, the thudding of hoofs sounded more loudly. In a few minutes a blur of fast moving shadows appeared on the trail.

'Cover me, Sam,' Bellamy said, moving out to the middle of the trail.

The horses were almost on top of him before the riders saw his dimly outlined figure. They reined in sharply.

A voice said: 'What the hell — '

Bellamy called out: 'Hold it, everyone. Don't try anything smart. Who are you an' where're you heading?'

Someone called back: 'I'll put a slug through you, then we'll know where *you're* headin'.'

There were a few laughs at the sally.

Bellamy called: 'Seems to me I know that voice. Sounds like a deputy I met in Durango. I guess you're way outa your territory, feller. Anyway, come forward an' let's have a look at you.'

A horseman came slowly towards Bellamy and stopped a yard away from him. The man peered forward.

'Well, dog my cats, if it ain't that two-gun totin' hoss licker that druv for Holden.' He got down from his horse. 'Sweney's the name, feller, deputy sheriff of Durango like you said. What you doin' here, Bellamy?'

'You tell first.' Bellamy's voice still had an edge to it.

'Come to collect a feller named Kerney. Guess you know him all right, an' from what I heard from Lin Jones, he ain't no friend of yourn.'

'You've got that part right,' Bellamy answered. 'But what're you hunting Kerney for, an' why so far off your own stamping ground? Seems to me when I was in Durango, you went out of your way to make me know for certain that this part was way out of your territory.'

'Makes a difference when a man's wanted for doin' a killin' in Durango.'

'Kerney wanted for a killin'? You'd better tell your men to get down off their hosses an' rest a spell. Kerney ain't been anywhere up this way. 'Least, not in any known parts.'

Sweney turned and called: 'OK, fellers. Here's where we breakfast.'

He walked towards the camp with Bellamy while the four riders who had made up the rest of the posse trailed behind him. Observing the camp, which was just coming to life in the growing dawn, Sweney said:

'What's all this, Bellamy. Starting a land trek?'

Bellamy told him how Kerney had gained possession of the town and stage line. He hesitated a moment before telling of the reputed gold mine — even to a deputy sheriff, the mention of gold could be a very bad thing — but at this stage, there was no alternative.

Sweney whistled. 'Dern pity there ain't any gold, but of all the low down, lousy coyotes, that buzzard Kerney sure wants some beatin'. Pity we couldn't catch up with him at Smethers' place, which was what we reckoned on doing. If we could have caught him there an' got him back to Durango we'da had him hung before anyone started an argument 'bout whose territory he was catched on. The law sure moves fast in Durango.'

Sam, who up to now had trailed alongside without saying a word said: 'This killing that Kerney did in Durango — when did it happen? I can't figure out how he got to Durango an' yet seemed to be round Red Rock most of the time.'

Sweney hesitated for a moment. 'Guess you fellers'll find out the truth some time. Kerney didn't actually do this killin'. You heard how Holden was shot in a saloon brawl. Well, we kinda liked Holden and did our best to find out who plugged him. We got around to suspectin' a no-good bum called Ratty Perkins, an' figured a little pressure would make him talk. It didn't work out that way. Ratty pulled a gun but he wasn't slick enough. I got him first. When Ratty realized he was dying he got real nasty and talked plenty, more than enough to tell us Kerney had paid him to do the job on Holden. As I said, we liked Holden, so figured to pull Kerney into our own territory where we could hang him without any trouble.'

Bellamy's mouth tightened. 'Don't worry none about Kerney. I'll save you the trouble of hanging him. Let's get some breakfast into us an' get these wagons rolling again. The sooner I see these folks safe in Durango the sooner I can 'tend to Kerney.'

Sweney booted a stone that lay in his path. 'I gotta say somethin' that'll sound bad to you. Me an' the boys'd sure like to join up with you but you know how it is. We're well out of our own territory now, an' the State gets kinda tough on sheriffs stampin' around outside their own backyard. We'd sort of figured to catch up with Kerney when no one was lookin' but now, with all these folks knowin' — '

Bellamy gave him a grin. 'Say no more, feller. I guess you've got to keep more or less inside the law. There's one thing you could do though. You an' your boys see these folks into Durango while I get after that pole-cat myself.'

Sweney gave a dismal grunt. 'Sure, we'll do that. Hate missin' all the fun though.' His mouth widened into a grin. 'Say, I could give myself a vacation. Ain't never had a vacation afore. Yep, that's it. I send the boys back with these folks an' they can tell my boss I'm on vacation.'

He grinned even wider as he unpinned his badge.

11

Since his abortive attempt to kill Bellamy, Kerney felt like a gambler who had staked all on the spin of the wheel and was now waiting to see which number the ball would drop into. Time after time he cursed his hastiness in sending the miners into Red Rock before making sure that Bellamy was dead. Now, it must be plain to Bellamy what he himself was after, and Kerney judged that Bellamy would not rest from trying to grab the gold for himself. It was now more important than ever that Bellamy should die.

Several other things worried Kerney. There was this nomad life he was living. For since he had failed in his attempt on Bellamy's life he had thought it wise to clear away from Smethers' shack and camp in the open some miles away from the trail. Joe Sangers, his old barkeep, was with him, having joined him just as he was coming away from the Smethers' place. Sangers was both a major prop and source of further worry to Kerney. Without Sangers' skilled cooking and ability to make comfort out of comparative hardship, Kerney felt he would hardly have been able to endure the loss of the comforts he had been used to for so long. Yet at times, when he had surprised Sangers in a sidelong glance at him, he wondered if this last henchman of his was not really another man to be feared.

Sangers had been a party to his scheming right from the beginning. In fact, Sangers had suggested the elimination of Zeke, once Zeke had ceased to be useful. Now, Kerney was calculating, not if he should rid himself of Sangers, but how soon.

Sangers also had ideas on the subject of elimination, but as yet they were vague. He had been into Red Rock that morning, sent by Kerney to assess what had been happening. Consequently,

Kerney knew of the evacuation of the town. Sangers had learned one other thing, but made no mention of his knowledge to Kerney. The shooting of Dolly Smethers had given Sangers much to think about, for it had not taken much pondering on his part to lay the blame for the murder on Kerney's shoulders. Sangers knew how things had been between Dolly and Kerney, and Kerney now appeared in a different light. Kerney, the man who could scheme, and manage it so others did his fighting and killing, was a man to be feared, but Kerney with the murder of a woman on his hands was somebody entirely different. But there was Bellamy to be reckoned with too. He could not be caught and hanged for murder, and Sangers licked lips that were dry with fear at the thought of trying to get Bellamy with a gun. He concluded that he would not be able to make any move until Bellamy was out of the way.

Kerney's thoughts on that point were

exactly the same. But Kerney did not propose to wait on Bellamy's coming — he was going to be in Red Rock waiting for him. By Kerney's reckoning, Bellamy should now be approaching Durango, keeping careful guard over his two-wagon train. That meant that Bellamy could not possibly get back to Red Rock before tomorrow's nightfall. There was, however, a chance that Bellamy would not ride all the way to Durango. He might, in fact, double back when he reached the Smethers' place. Well, Kerney himself could be in Red Rock in a couple of hours, ample time in which to lay the trap that Bellamy would have to ride into.

Kerney pulled a smouldering piece of wood from the camp fire and put it to the end of the cigar on which he had been chewing for the last half-hour.

'Saddle two horses,' he said briefly. 'We'll ride into Red Rock and see how those miners are getting on.'

'What about Bellamy?' Sangers ventured.

'Leave that to me. I'll fix him.'

Sangers saddled up in silence and rode behind Kerney until they arrived at Red Rock. There, he sat his mount while Kerney heaved himself to the ground and talked with the foreman.

The men had still not quite cleared the site of debris left by the fire but most of the rock formation now showed. Sangers expected Kerney to be annoyed at the slow pace of the men's progress but he seemed more interested in the kegs of blasting powder and the methods that would be used for firing charges, asking numerous questions about lengths of fuse and the time they took to burn. Finally, Kerney excused all his questioning by saying that he had another spot in mind that looked as if it might be gold bearing but wanted to experiment privately before turning men on the job.

The foreman grinned. 'Don't blame you for trying to keep a strike quiet. There'll be plenty after it as soon as it gets known. Me, I'd sooner make steady dough this way, seen plenty of fellers chasin' after gold that was always somewhere else.'

Kerney gave an expansive laugh and clapped his hand on the foreman's shoulder. 'Guess it could be that way with me. Anyway I'll take a keg of powder and a length of fuse and try my luck.'

'It's your powder,' the foreman laughed back. 'You'd better take a pick an' spade an' things with you too.'

Sangers climbed down from his mount and helped to load the selected gear behind their saddles. That done, he followed Kerney along the deserted street of the town until they reached the farther end and could look down the trail towards Durango. In the heat of the afternoon sun Kerney had him dig a hole right in the middle of the street. A hole a yard wide and about the same depth. In it the keg of powder was placed with a length of fuse attached to it. Kerney himself took the other end of the fuse to the side of one of the shacks then superintended the covering of the keg — first, with large rocks that nearly filled the hole then, with dirt and dust gathered from the heap Sangers had dug. He saw to it that the place where the digging had been done matched up with the remainder of the rutted street before leaving the place. The rest, as he informed Sangers, consisted of sitting and waiting in concealment until Bellamy showed up.

The two took up positions in an empty shack and, turn about, watched the trail through a broken and dirty window. Kerney smoked cigar after cigar in the stifling heat of the shack, seemingly unaffected either by the warmth of the place or the tremendous fug made by his cigars. Sangers chewed and spat tobacco juice incessantly, and when it was not his turn for watching the trail, moved restlessly about the narrow confines of the place.

The sun had almost dipped and was sending long, torrid rays along the length of the trail when Sangers grunted something about needing fresh air and went out of doors. Kerney made no comment, as the door of the cabin did not front directly on to the street. It was in his mind that it would suit his purpose very well if Sangers was somewhere else than in the shack when Bellamy put in an appearance. Somewhere near the keg of powder, for instance. In fact, he meditated several times whether or not to put a bullet through Sangers' back and dump his body out of sight somewhere within range of the coming explosion. It would be nice to dispose of both Bellamy and Sangers at the one time and by the one means. He decided, with regret, to play careful until the end. After all, there was no guarantee that Bellamy would come seeking himself on this or any other night and until Bellamy was finished with, Sangers might still be of use.

Sangers, outside and in the comparative coolness of the shade cast by the shack next to the one they were using, found his eyes continually attracted to the end of the fuse. The white, cord-like substance looked innocent and malevolent at one and the same time. If there was some way in which he could deal with Kerney at about the same time that the fuse was lit, some way that could make his death seem like the result of the explosion — Suddenly, he stopped chewing, spat out the wad, fished in his back pocket for his plug of tobacco and, as he bit off a fresh plug, let a slow smile travel over his plump, oily face. He went into the shack again and relieved Kerney at the chore of watching, content now to watch the purpling shadows creep over the trail.

Kerney did not fail to notice the change that had come over Sangers, and grinned to himself in the near darkness of the shack. Sangers, he thought, had some little scheme of his own. Some idea of making a grab on his own behalf. Kerney almost chuckled at the idea of Sangers trying to outsmart him. Only one man had come anywhere near to that and —

Sangers' voice cut short his thought. 'There's two of 'em, boss.'

Kerney hurried to the window. Almost a mile down the trail two riders showed clearly in the fast fading light.

Sangers made a move towards the door but Kerney's hand reached out to detain him.

'Not yet. There's plenty of time. We've got to be certain it is Bellamy, whoever the other feller is.'

Sangers gave a grunt and settled by the window again. He was certain the man on the right was Bellamy and, like Kerney, didn't care much who his companion was. He waited another few minutes and again made a move towards the door.

This time Kerney rapped out. 'Stay where you are. I'll tell you when it's time to move.'

Sangers halted, sweat breaking out on his forehead. Had Kerney devined his thoughts? He checked the idea — impossible. Thoughts were thoughts and could not be read by any man.

Besides, Kerney had no reason to suspect him. All he had to do was keep quiet and watch his opportunity when they were both outside.

Kerney straightened up from the window. 'You watch,' he said shortly. 'Tell me when they get in line with that second tree.'

Sangers crouched by the window watching the slow approach of the two riders. After a moment he gave a half turn of his head to tell Kerney that he was now certain that Bellamy was one of the men. He got the words out but some odd cast of the shadows on Kerney's face made the sweat break out on him again. When he resumed watching it was with his head half turned so that Kerney was still in his view.

Presently Sangers stood up. 'They're just alongside the first tree now. I can't make out who the other guy is.'

Kerney shrugged. 'It doesn't matter. Let's get outside.'

The pair got to the angle of the shack

and Kerney took a cautious peep around the corner. After a few seconds he said:

'Get ready but don't light the fuse until I say, and the moment you do, run like hell.'

Sangers bent down by the fuse, now almost invisible in the dusk. He groped with his left hand for matches while his right hand assured himself that the Derringer he had stuffed in his belt was loose. He gave a glance upwards at Kerney, expectant of the word, and just in time, dodged the downwards swing of Kerney's Colt. Desperately, Sangers dived at Kerney's knees. The big man floundered and fell heavily, almost crushing the breath out of Sangers who, with the fear of death upon him, fought madly to claw himself free of Kerney's enormous weight. Several times he made the big man grunt with pain as he drove either fist or foot at him but still Kerney held the ascendancy. Then sheer fright gave Sanger the idea of gouging Kerney's eyes. With supreme effort he got his hand to Kerney's face and jabbed thumb and forefinger into his eyes. Kerney bounded up with a scream of pain and as he came to his feet kicked blindly at the man he saw only vaguely through his streaming eyes. His first kick landed squarely in Sangers' face bringing a gush of blood. The other kicks landed on ribs, in the stomach or anywhere else that chanced to be in the way.

Sangers went down and lay still. Kerney saw his form as something distant and veiled through the anguish of his eyes. Jibbering and cursing he got to the ground and groped around for one of the dropped weapons. His hand closed on the Derringer and, still half blinded with tears, he stood over Sangers, put the muzzle of the gun to his head and pressed the trigger.

Before the echoes had died down Kerney was round the back of the shack, fumbling to get his foot in a stirrup then, half in and half out of the saddle, he hit for the open ground outside the town.

Bellamy jerked his mount to a halt as the shot boomed out. He and Sweney had entered the town and were alert for anything.

Sweney said: 'That Kerney havin' a blast at you, do you reckon?'

'If he is, he's changed his ideas of weapons. Last time it was a Winchester — that sounded like an old Derringer. No, sir, I don't reckon that was Kerney's doin'. 'Sides, we've kept too much in the shadow to make a decent target. 'Nother thing. I didn't hear no slug go by.'

'Uh huh. I reckon you're right on all points. How if we split and take a mosey round? Sounded to me to come from over by those shacks.'

'Yeah, you cover the street. I'll take round the backs of the shacks. I know round there better'n you do.'

He swung his mount into the space between the saloon and the hotel and slid from the saddle, leaving the reins trailing. Stumbling a little over the uneven ground he passed to the backs of the buildings. As he reached them there came the distant drumming of galloping hoofs. Someone, he reflected, had had the sense to walk a horse quietly away from the place before putting it to a gallop. There was small hope of following in the dark and he would have gone back to where Sweney was waiting had he not caught the sound of the restless movements of another horse somewhere around. Sliding one of the Colts from its holster he continued his groping search of the backs and spaces between the shacks, coming round each building angle with caution, expecting that at any moment a gun would cut loose at him. The last of the row of shacks reached, he moved down its side toward the street and saw the sprawled out figure that was Sangers.

Straightening up from his brief examination of the body he called softly to Sweney and told him what he had found.

Sweney fumbled around in the dark trying to find out what had happened.

'Could sure use a light here, Jeff,' he grumbled.

'Wouldn't do. Might be other jaspers around, although I don't reckon so. Reckon we'll just have to wait 'til daylight.'

'Yeah, I guess you're right. Might as well get the hosses an' fix ourselves comfortable in the shack.'

They brought their mounts and also the horse Bellamy had discovered and hitched them close to the shack, then took turns at watching and sleeping until first light.

Sweney was watching when the coming dawn made it possible to see details. He called into the shack.

'Hey, Jeff. Lookee here.'

Bellamy came out and Sweney pointed first, to a Colt lying on the ground, then to a box of spilled sulphur matches.

'Looks like this guy was lookin' for somethin' when he got his,' Sweney said.

Bellamy picked up the Colt. 'Kerney's. I know those silver mountings. Ain't been fired either. The dead guy is Joe Sangers, Kerney's barkeep. Thought it was him last night, but couldn't be certain, it bein' so plumb dark.'

He moved closer to Sangers' body, stretched face downwards, the fingers apparently clutching at earth.

'This feller was slugged, mebbe with the butt of this gun, then afterwards shot. Look, there's powder burns on the side of his face. Weren't shot with a six-gun either, take a Derringer or somethin' — yeah, the Derringer we heard last night — to make a hole like that. Hey, what's this underneath him? Give me a lift with him.'

They lifted the corpse to one side and Bellamy picked up the end of the fuse. A few seconds later they had followed its course to the middle of the street. A brief search discovered the spade that had been used to dig the hole and a few seconds work uncovered the keg of powder.

Sweney wiped sweat from his fore-head, sweat that was not entirely caused by his exertions with the spade.

'By hell, — Jeff, I've run into some things, but no one's ever tried to blast me to glory with gunpowder before.'

Bellamy grinned a tight lipped grin. 'Me neither. The sooner we catch up with Kerney the better. He's got altogether too many ideas for my liking. One thing, I know where he got the blastin' powder from. Let's take it along an' see the gents that provided it. Mebbe they've got ideas as well.'

With a keg of powder lashed on the saddle of the spare horse they rode up to the miner's camp. Breakfast was just about over when they arrived but a smell of coffee and bacon still lingered in the air.

The foreman got to his feet on seeing Bellamy. He started with a friendly, if nervous, greeting then his eyes took in the keg of powder and his mouth closed on the words.

Bellamy regarded him in silence for a

few moments, then he jerked a thumb in the direction of the powder keg. 'What do you know about this, feller?'

The foreman hesitated. 'Not much. Looks like the same keg Kerney took.'

'Anyone with Kerney?'

'Yeah, a kinda oily looking guy, sort of fattish an' had black hair. Kerney didn't say his name but I took it he worked for Kerney.'

Bellamy heaved himself from the saddle. 'Guess you can relax, an' if there's any of that bacon an' coffee left me an' Sweney could sure use it.'

The foreman moved with such readiness to the cook fire that Sweney grinned at Bellamy as he climbed down from his mount.

The other men, who had been watching with some apprehension, moved off as the foreman poured coffee and forked bacon on to two plates.

Bellamy said, after he had chewed a few mouthfuls:

'If I were you, feller, I wouldn't have those men of yours use too much time on this job. I don't reckon you're goin' to get paid for it somehow.'

The foreman gave him a startled look. 'As how? I don't get your meanin'. Kerney gave us a pretty good advance on the job an' promised regular payments as we went on.'

Bellamy took a swallow of coffee. 'Take my advice an' clear out. Any time Kerney shows up here, he's a dead man. I want him for two murders an' several other things, including tryin' to blast me off the earth with that keg of powder.'

'We've got nothin' to do with it. Honest.'

'Sure, I know that, you wouldn't be talking now if you had. Just tell me one thing, then take my advice an' quit the place. You've been around a lot of minin' projects I guess. See anythin' here that makes you think there's a rich strike?'

The foreman laughed. 'Rich strike! There ain't any kind of a strike. By what I've seen the natural lie of the rock has taken more than a beatin' at some time. You can see over there where the strata has made some kind of a side slip. Could be that it's buried itself a coupla mile down, mebbe more. Even if we ever got to it, there's no guarantee that the vein Kerney has been following hasn't been busted wide apart.'

'Could it be then, that a guy, say some guy a good many years back, could have turned up a sizable piece of ore here that assayed pretty good?'

'Oh, sure, that's the kind of thing that happens all the time. A feller has the luck to fall over a chunk that mebbe fetches him a hundred bucks. Then he goes mad an' digs the country for miles around an' nary another grain.' He grinned. 'That's why fellers like us'd sooner dig for regular pay.'

Bellamy answered his grin. 'Thanks for confirming what someone else told me about the place. Sorry your job has to fold up, but that's the way it is.'

The foreman gave him a searching look. 'You don't have to feel sorry for us, Mister. I'm derned sorry fer anyone like you that has to mix it with a gold-crazy murderer.'

12

The miners had gone, taking what they could on the single wagon that was left to them and caching the remainder of their gear, to be collected later. The hot afternoon sun poured down on a deserted street, while a lazy, dust-stirring wind swung loose doors or gently rattled a clapboard that had pulled from its fastenings. The settled melancholy of the place affected Bellamy and Sweney more than had the job of burying Sangers. They had, by mutual consent, made their headquarters in the saloon and had found a few bottles of beer in the litter of the place.

Sweney emptied the mug he was using and set it down: 'What's next, Jeff, do we set here an' wait for Kerney to come or do we scour around for him?'

Bellamy considered for a moment:

'Been trying to figure that myself. Seems to me we might sit here for ever an' Kerney mightn't come. On the other hand we ain't got much of an idea where to look for him. If we go he's liable to slip in an' hive down somewhere an' mebbe wait for us with a scatter gun or somethin'. It's kinda hard to reckon what he will do.'

'If I was Kerney,' Sweney said thoughtfully. 'I'd get somewhere where I could watch the trail to Durango. That way I'd know who was in this town.'

'Sounds reasonable, an' if Kerney's doin' that he'll know his miners have quit an' there's only me an' you here.' He straightened up suddenly. 'Say, Kerney ain't any slouch at thinkin' things out. He'll be as far ahead with his ideas as we are. He'll reckon that sooner or later I'll get tired of sittin' around. Mebbe even get tired enough to quit on the job, if so, I'd head for Durango, seein' as the trails in the other direction don't go any place worthwhile. Yep, if I were Kerney, I'd hive down somewhere this side of the Smethers' place, right handy to that big chunk of rock where another buzzard tried to dry-gulch me.'

Sweney poured another bottle of beer. 'That bein' so, we'd best set here two or three days until he gets good an' tired of watchin' then go out some night an' get the murderin' skunk.'

Bellamy drank without answering and remained silent for so long that eventually Sweney said:

'Hey, what the heck's eatin' you? You look like someone's jumped your claim or somethin'.'

Bellamy looked at him sour faced: 'I just got to remembering what I came here for an' I'll never know the answer. Dorlen's death could have been an accident. Mebbe I oughta get some sense an' clear out. Kerney's goin' to be a disappointed man anyway when he finds his gold mine is only ordinary dirt an' rock.'

'There's all the other men Kerney had put underground one way and another. Someone ought to make him pay for that.'

'Ain't no way of payin' for dead men,' Bellamy grunted.

'There's the folks he druv out of town.'

'Shucks, they'll likely do better in Durango than in a dump like this. Lots of men would have quit the place before if they'd had enough push behind them.'

'Like that old feller, Sam an' the gal you told me about, what's her name — Susan or somethin'?'

Bellamy jumped to his feet: 'Aw, shurrup. I'll stay an' clean up on that skunk Kerney, if that's what you want.'

Sweney grinned then whistled softly as Bellamy stamped sullenly towards the door to stand on the veranda.

He found the next three days of Bellamy's varying moods trying in the extreme but somehow put up with them cheerfully.

On the afternoon of the third day both men were lounging in the sun.

They came alert at the same moment to the sound of horse hoofs.

'Coming at a fast clip,' Bellamy said after listening intently.

'Yeah, sure is, an' only one hoss. Kerney must have decided to try an' stampede us.'

Bellamy shook his head: 'Don't seem to me like Kerney's way of actin', however if it is — '

He picked up the Winchester and checked on the loading. A few minutes later a rider came into sight. Bellamy put down the rifle with a surprised: 'Sam Moss, by heck. What the tarnation brings him?'

The pair jumped from the veranda into the street and stood in the path of the oncoming horse. Sam, who had been belabouring the horse unmercifully, reined in with difficulty and floundered awkwardly from the saddle. Bellamy saw that he was almost at the end of his endurance and slid an arm round his shoulders to support him. Helped by Sweney he got him into the saloon and on to a chair. Sweney found spirits of some kind and gave them to the gasping man. Sam choked and spluttered but in a moment or two managed to say:

'Susan, Kerney's got hold of her, he's mad, he'll kill her — '

Bellamy got the gist of Sam's story. For some reason, not quite clear to him, Sam and Susan had decided to return to Red Rock. They had found the Smethers' place empty and decided to stop there over night. Kerney had surprised them but they had felt no reason to be afraid of him. Then Kerney had whipped out a gun and told Sam that if he wanted Susan to live he was to ride to Red Rock and persuade Bellamy and Sweney into riding out to meet him.

Sam looked a completely broken man. He raised a haggard face to Bellamy: 'Jeff, it's a trap to kill you, an' mebbe my girl as well. She'll know too much for him to let her go.' He moaned and rocked in his chair. 'My God, Jeff, it's all my fault. I guessed what Kerney was up to long ago an' could have stopped it if I'd had the guts to speak out. My God, Jeff, what can we do?'

Bellamy snapped: 'Do! We've got to get movin' pronto, me and Sweney.' He accepted without question that Sweney would ride with him. 'You, Sam, stay here an' get rested. Don't try ridin' after us 'cause we can't afford to have any one that ain't good an' fit. Which you ain't. Now don't worry none, that Kerney's a smart guy but Sweney an' me's got ideas as well.'

The pair left five minutes later and immediately put their horses to a gallop.

Sweney said as they pounded along: 'Be about sundown when we get there, Jeff.'

'I know, I aim to make it while there's still some light.'

'Hope the horses last out at that pace.'

After that both men settled down to hard riding and exchanged not a single word as the dusty miles passed beneath them. They gave their mounts five minutes blow at the first stage halt and as they mounted again Sweney said:

'You got any ideas yet, Jeff?'

'No, not beyond tearing the skunk in half with my bare hands. You can bet he'll make us drop our guns before he lets us get close to him.'

Sweney's shoulders hunched. It seemed to him Kerney had won and they were both riding to their deaths. Using Susan as a hostage, Kerney could practically force the pair of them to come within gun range and then — Sweney bent to his riding. If Bellamy could take it, he supposed he himself could, but it would be tough to go down without being able to grab for a gun.

Bellamy's thoughts were different. He was certain that if he could not somehow outsmart Kerney, Susan Moss as well as Sweney and himself would die. The thought came to him grimly that, had he pulled out of the game none of them would have been in danger at this moment and Kerney would have been a bitterly disappointed man as regards the gold. It just showed where a guy could get himself and others when he put sentiment before hard fact. Of course he liked the girl, liked her a heck of a lot. Liked old Sam as well for that matter. But tarnation, there were other folks he liked without getting shot up about it. He straightened in the saddle. Perhaps he hadn't liked others quite so much. That Kerney was a real louse, he ought to die. Goddam it, he just had to die.

Bellamy beat his brains afresh for a workable scheme to defeat Kerney, then within three miles of the Smethers' place shouted to Sweney: 'Hey, pull up, I got some kind of an idea.'

Sweney reined in his lathered mount: 'What sort of an idea?'

Bellamy's lips twisted into a mirthless grin: 'A hell of an idea. Listen, we'll have to come to Kerney without our guns.'

Sweney nodded: 'You can bet he'll make it that way.'

'Well, there's other things besides

guns. Good job you always have a blanket roll an' such behind your saddle. Unhitch it, will you?'

Sweney got down from the saddle and spread his gear on the ground. 'There you are, but I'm derned if I know what you can get out of it.'

'Pass me that axe an' that hog-tie.'

Sweney handed him a small axe and a length of cord then grinned as Bellamy hitched the cord to the handle of the axe and slung it over his shoulder so that the axe was at his back. The loose end of the cord, Bellamy threaded under his belt so that it would come away with a jerk of his hand.

Sweney repacked his gear and mounted: 'Kerney's in for one hell of a surprise,' he commented as they moved off again.

Another ten minutes of hard riding brought them within sight of the stage buildings and both men eased their mounts to a walk. Kerney would undoubtedly be watching for them and signal them to stop.

They were within five hundred

yards of the place when a gun boomed, the smoke from it showing from the doorway of the shack, then Kerney's voice ordered them to leave horses and gunbelts where they were before walking forward.

Bellamy said quietly as they dropped their gunbelts: 'Remember exactly where these guns are, partner. We might need them in a dern big hurry.'

He raised his arms and started towards the shack.

Sweney said: 'I'll remember all right, if I live long enough.' He too raised his arms and walked level with Bellamy and a few feet to Bellamy's left.

Fifty yards from the shack, Kerney showed himself at the door, pushing Susan in front of him into the open.

Bellamy murmured: 'We've got to get closer than this, feller.' He lengthened his stride but Kerney called on them to halt.

The gun in Kerney's hand, directed at Susan, gave them no alternative but to obey.

Bellamy muttered: 'He's bound to have us closer in if he wants to plug us both.'

'I feel plenty close already,' Sweney whispered.

Kerney seemed to be hesitating, then, as if his mind was made up, he shouted: 'I'll make a deal, come closer — no tricks or else the girl gets a slug in the back.'

'He's playin' it our way,' Sweney murmured as they moved forward.

'Got to make him move his gun-hand some way 'fore I can make a move, an' he wants us close in so he can't miss when he turns the hardware on us.'

Kerney halted them again when they were twenty feet from him: 'Surprise for you eh, Bellamy, and your friend whoever he is?'

'Got one for you too,' Bellamy said tonelessly. 'Your mine ain't worth a plugged nickel.'

Kerney gave a little jump, then laughed: 'You won't get at me that way, Bellamy.'

Bellamy turned towards Sweney: 'Ain't it the derndest thing? You tell a guy the truth about somethin' that oughta interest him an' he comes near to callin' you a liar.'

Kerney cackled: 'A good try, Bellamy, but it won't do. Now you and your friend listen carefully because they're the last words you're going to hear. I reckon you were clever enough to guess what might happen when I got you here. Well I won't disappoint you. I'm going to shoot both of you.'

'I wouldn't be fool enough to shoot a deputy from Durango, if I were you, Kerney, not for a gold mine that ain't. Show him your badge, Sweney.'

Sweney's hand went towards his shirt pocket. Instantly, Kerney's weapon came round to bear in his direction.

Bellamy also made a move, a move so rapid that hand and arm were a blur. Out of the blurred movement the axe whirled at Kerney, glinting in the sun's rays as it pivoted in its flight. As Kerney fired, Sweney and Bellamy dived for the ground. Kerney gave a howl of pain and staggered backwards. Bellamy came from the ground in a plunging run, grabbed at Susan and flung her round the angle of the shack. Sweney made a crabbing movement to one side then flattened as a volley of shots kicked dirt all around him. Bellamy rocketed round to the front of the shack again, scooped up the fallen axe and buried its blade deep in the door that Kerney was just slamming shut. Bellamy ripped out a curse, charged the stout door with his shoulder, then quickly decided he was acting foolishly. The thing to do now was to get Susan and themselves out of gun range.

He grabbed Susan by the arm and raced with her towards the barn with Sweney just on their heels. A crash of breaking glass as Kerney poked a rifle through a window added speed to their feet and they tumbled into the barn just as a badly aimed slug whined by.

Gasping for breath, Sweney asked: 'An' what next? Seems to me that guy'll get around to rememberin' we ain't got our guns. If he rushes us now I reckon it's all up.'

'Kerney's hurt some,' Bellamy said. 'But I don't know how bad. Thing is, he can't be in two places at once. You take Susan up into the hay loft. I'm goin' to make a run for our hardware.'

'You'll never make it. It's all open ground. Kerney's able to hold a rifle, he'll get you as easy as pickin' off a settin' hen.'

'Help Susan into the loft. It's the only safe place seein' we can't bar the barn door on the inside. I'll dodge Kerney somehow.'

As he moved to the door, Susan sprang towards him, her hands seeking to detain him: 'Jeff, you'll be killed. You haven't got a chance.'

He shook her off roughly: 'Got to make a chance.'

The barn door was nearly closed, Sweney having dragged it to as they entered. Bellamy now pushed it open an inch at a time in the hope that

Kerney would not see the small movement. The narrow beam of light widened to a foot, to two feet then Kerney's rifle cracked and a slug screamed past Bellamy's face. He dragged the door shut again just as two more slugs tore through the planking.

'We told you how it'd be,' Sweney said. 'Now let's all get up in the loft. We might stand a chance when it gets good an' dark.'

Susan was already in the loft and Sweney on the foot of the ladder. Bellamy had almost to grope his way to reach them, so faint was the light that now came through cracks and spaces between the boards of the barn. As he reached Sweney he heard the thud of the bar dropping into its sockets across the door. Kerney had made sure they did not rush out. Bellamy struck a match, there was no reason against having a light if he could find a lamp. He found one after striking two more matches and lit it. As the flame flared up a horse nickered from the deepest recesses of the barn. Bellamy breathed unspoken curses. If he had remembered that Kerney must have a mount somewhere, he would have had a good chance of bursting into the open. Now the bar was on the door and it was too late.

Sweney said: 'I hear we've got a hoss anyway.'

Susan was climbing down from the loft. She laughed, a trifle hysterically, Bellamy thought. It came to him that she was taking the whole business very bravely. To keep up her spirits further, he said:

'Soon as it gets real dark we'll burst through the door an' ride that hoss out. If he's good enough for Kerney's weight, he'll carry us three.'

Sweney cackled, Bellamy thought the sound far from genuine. Probably Sweney had got to figuring Kerney's next move, as he himself had done — kerosene spilt round the outside of the place and a match put to it.

Kerney didn't even have to bother

about a mount. Bellamy's own and Sweney's were outside somewhere.

Half an hour passed before Bellamy caught the first, faint whiff of kerosene. Immediately he rolled and lit a cigarette, hoping that the tobacco smell would keep that of kerosene from Susan. Sweney also made himself a smoke.

Susan looked from one to the other: 'That's kerosene I can smell isn't it? Kerney's going to set fire to the barn.'

Bellamy saw she was having difficulty in controlling herself. 'I reckon so, Sue,' he said quietly. 'But if he does, Sweney an' me ain't goin' to sit here an' let you roast. There's an old wagon shaft over in the corner an' come the first whiff of smoke we'll ram the door open with it. The longer we wait the darker it'll be outside an' the better chance we'll have of scatterin'.'

Another ten minutes passed in silence. Bellamy wondered at first why Kerney delayed starting the fire then thought that he had first gone to catch one of the horses. That might take him some time as neither horse handled easily. He changed his mind about waiting for it to grow darker and said to Sweney:

'Let's try bustin' this door now, Kerney don't seem to be around.'

'Sure, anythin's better'n settin' an' doin' nothin'.'

They picked up the wagon shaft, a heavy one, and ran it full tilt against the door. The timbers shuddered under the impact and on a second ram a plank cracked.

'Three or four more bumps, mebbe,' Sweney grunted.

As they drew back for another charge the first curls of smoke seeped into the place and a volley of shots ripping through the door made them drop the shaft and jump to one side.

'That was a six-gun,' Bellamy growled. 'And he fired four shots.'

He picked up the shaft again and slammed it against the door then leapt aside as two more slugs tore through the woodwork.

'Gun's empty now Sweney, three or four more good slams, an' we're out.'

'Yeah — if he ain't got the Winchester handy.'

They battered at the door again and this time the ram was nearly through before the gun barked again but now smoke was pouring in through the splintered door, filling the place with choking fumes.

'We gotta have that door bust, gun or no gun,' Bellamy coughed.

They rammed at the door once more and again came a volley of shots. Bellamy counted mentally, six, seven, eight, then realized that only two of the slugs had come through the door.

'Break out,' he bawled. 'We got friends outside.'

As they rammed again and again at the door the shooting outside came in oddly spaced, single shots. The horse at the back of the barn started a shrill scream of fear as more and more smoke billowed into the place then the door finally split wide enough for a man to get through. Bellamy scrambled out and yanked savagely at the bar that was still holding, then swung the shattered door wide on its hinges. He shouted to Sweney to get Susan out of sight somewhere then plunged into the dense smoke for the terror stricken horse. He came out of the barn hanging on the animal's head rope, then flung himself on its back with a giant leap.

Somewhere to his right a gun boomed and flashed red. Who was firing it he had no idea and felt himself naked without a weapon to join in the proceedings. He let the horse tear across the open ground, then unable to check it, flung himself from its back. He rolled once or twice then sat up to find just where he was. Dancing flames licking at the sides of the barn, showed how far he had come. The flash and roar of two guns near at hand told of two men conducting a battle. One of them must be Kerney, but which? Bellamy stood up and tried to locate his mount. He did not whistle it to come to him, for its position was the only thing he had to indicate where his guns lay. Then he caught the dim outline of both mounts standing quietly together close to where one of the guns flashed. He started to run across the intervening space and was within fifty yards of the horses when a bulky figure seemed to come from the ground almost at the side of the animals. Bellamy halted and there was nothing for it but to put his fingers to his lips and send out a piercing whistle to bring his own mount to him. At the shrill sound the animal turned instantly and started to move towards him, but by that time the bulky figure he had seen was struggling to climb into the saddle of Sweney's horse. Bellamy heard cursing in a voice he recognized, then Kerney was spurring towards him.

He went to ground a second before horse and rider reached him and felt the hot sting of a slug ripping across his neck as Kerney rode past. There came two more shots fired backwards as

Kerney galloped away into the darkness. The blood flowing from Bellamy's wound went unheeded as he reached for the reins of his own dancing mount and he was not five hundred yards behind Kerney when the roan began to gather speed.

In the first moments of the pursuit Bellamy spurred his mount to its best speed, then he remembered he was without a weapon of any kind. Kerney, though flying from him at the moment could still choose the spot to stop and fight. For once Bellamy had to content himself with just hanging on. One thing, it could not be for long. Both horses had already done a hard ride that day. If they lasted to Red Rock that would be their limit.

For almost half an hour the roan kept its pace then Bellamy felt it falter in its stride. It picked up again and a few minutes later made another staggering stride. Bellamy immediately pulled the animal into a walk. He could see Kerney ahead though rather dimly and he wondered how the mount he was riding was managing to carry his weight for so long at such a killing pace. A moment later he saw Kerney's height suddenly shorten. His over-driven mount had collapsed completely. Bellamy thought of encouraging his own horse to something of a trot though the animal was blowing badly and its head dropping, but the boom of Kerney's gun and the whistle of a spent slug told him that Kerney was on his feet again. Bellamy slid from his own saddle. There was no need for him to burden a gallant horse any longer. He went forward, like Kerney, on foot, his mount limping behind. Kerney blasted off two more shots — shots of a man too unnerved to wait for an easier target. Bellamy closed the distance at a run then went to ground as Kerney triggered off more shells. Then Kerney started to run — the heavy, ponderous trot of a big man who rarely took exercise.

Bellamy shouted a taunt. 'You're at the end of your rope, Kerney. Got one shot in your gun, ain't you? I'm comin' for you, Kerney. It'll take more'n one shot to put me down.'

Bellamy put on a burst of speed. Kerney tried to match it for a few seconds then turned and pointed the gun at Bellamy. Bellamy knew it was a trial of nerves. If he slackened his speed now Kerney would find nerve enough to hold the single shot that remained in the gun, might even gain some place where he could safely reload. Bellamy put on a greater spurt though the blood flowing from the wound in his neck seemed to be draining his strength.

At ten yards Kerney could stand it no longer. With an oath he pressed the trigger. Bellamy staggered as the slug scored his thigh, recovered his stride and before Kerney could turn to run threw himself upon him. For a minute they remained locked together each striving for a vital hold, then Bellamy hooked his foot behind Kerney's knee and sent him crashing to the ground. Bellamy came on top of his adversary grabbing for his throat. He found his hold and gripped hard. Then suddenly he was aware that Kerney no longer fought back. Kerney's weight, plus a boulder in the trail, had broken his back.

With a shudder of disgust Bellamy moved away and sank down heavily, weak and exhausted.

A week later Bellamy prepared to leave Red Rock. Some of the population had returned to the place and others were trickling in. Sweney came in that very morning bearing important news. The State of Colorado had belatedly discovered that Red Rock was within its boundaries and therefore under the jurisdiction of Durango.

'I got somethin' else to tell you too, Jeff,' Sweney said, his face downcast. 'The sheriff says you an' those guns of yours ain't welcome in a peaceful little place like Red Rock.'

'Peaceful little place!' laughed Bellamy. 'Well, I'll be gosh darned. But that's the way it goes. Sheriffs are all set on havin' a quiet existence. The law don't want fellers like me an' the bad men'll want us less.'

Sweney nodded. 'I guess you're right at that, Jeff. Say, did you ever find out just what that old buzzard Sam Moss had been up to?'

Bellamy grinned. 'Well — unofficially — '

'Sure, the past is the past.'

'Years ago Sam and another guy figured to salt a gold mine an' sell it.'

'You mean right here where Red Rock is now?'

'Yeah, right where Holden had his stage buildings. Sam got himself full of liquor an' talked too much before he an' his partner got the claim staked. Another guy jumps the place an' goes into Durango with most of the saltin's in a sack. This feller has some kind of fever which he dies of but before he died he blabbed about the claim.'

Sweney whistled. 'So another rush an' another lot of disappointed guys.'

'That's the way of it, an' meantime

Sam's partner is huntin' him with a gun on account of the dough they've lost on the deal. Sam actually caught sight of the guy when he made his last haul to Durango. Since then he's been scared to go near the place. When he was finally forced to leave Red Rock and go to Durango he found his old partner had died.'

'So that's what brought Sam back before the others?' Sweney grinned. 'That old so'n so. He was the only one in the place that was dead certain there was no gold in Red Rock.'

'Sure, an' on top of that Sam sees an easy openin' for himself in the freight business.'

Sweney chuckled, then said. 'How'd Kerney come in?'

'Hard to say, except that Sam says he an' his partner made a map of the claim an' that somehow it went missing. It's my guess that same map came into Kerney's hands.'

'Could be. Well, I'll be sorry to see you go, but I guess you've done all you want in Red Rock.'

'All except what I really came for,' eff said soberly. 'Well, I guess me an' the hoss'll get movin'.'

As he moved out of the empty shack he had been using, Susan appeared in the doorway. Sweney adroitly excused himself.

Susan said: 'I see you're ready to move off, Jeff.' She offered her hand. 'Well, it's been nice knowing you. Perhaps you'll be riding this way again. If so — ' She broke off abruptly.

'If so, I'll surely look up my friends — you and Sam.'

Susan gave him a searching look then turned and ran quickly from the shack.

Bellamy came outside. Sweney's face wore a puzzled frown.

'Somethin' worryin you?' asked Bellamy.

'Yeah, that gal, Susan. She ran from me like I was poison or somethin'.'

Bellamy did not answer for a moment, then he said quietly: 'She wasn't running from you, Sweney. I guess she was runnin' from me. A man that uses his guns ain't got no right to soft thoughts about any woman. That's one thing I've learned at any rate since I came to Red Rock.'

THE END